FOREVER TRAPPED

Megan,
You Rock!

FOREVER TRAPPED

INSPIRED BY "HOME BY THE SEA" BY GENESIS

PEGGY CHRISTIE

Copyright ©2022 by Peggy Christie

All rights reserved.

All characters in this book are fictitious. Any resemblance to any persons living, dead, or otherwise animated is strictly coincidental.

No part of this book may be reproduced in any form or by any electronic or mechanical means, including information storage and retrieval systems, without written permission from the author, except for the use of brief quotations in a book review.

Printed in the United States of America

Print ISBN 978-1-956824-00-1

Digital ISBN 978-1-956824-04-9

Dragon's Roost Press

207 Gardendale

Ferndale, MI 48220

thedragonsroost.biz

To my husband, Robert, for knowing the best way to introduce me to the genius of the band, Genesis, would be through their song with the creepiest premise.

To the members of Genesis - Tony Banks (lyricist), Phil Collins, and Mike Rutherford - for writing "Home by the Sea", the song that inspired these tales in the first place.

CONTENTS

Prologue	1
HARVEY HUDSPETH	13
(1900)	
SEBASTIAN BULLOCK	29
(Modern Day)	
MR. COPPERWELL	35
(1923)	
DANIEL WEAVER	49
(1984)	
ROSALIE	67
(Modern Day)	
MURIEL SPENCER	85
(1975)	
PETER and SALLY CONNERS	103
(1954)	
SYLVIA MATHESON	115
(1984)	
JONATHAN CRANE	129
(1695)	
PHIL HENDERSON	137
(Modern Day)	
Epilogue	151
About the Author	153
Also by Peggy Christie	155
About the Artist	157
Dragon's Roost Press	159

PROLOGUE

Travis elbowed Chuck in the ribs, goading him to walk up on the porch of the abandoned house. Chuck swiped at him with a half-empty beer bottle, slurring an angry response.

"Fuck, no. I ain't going up there. If you're so interested, why don't you go up? Hmm? I'll tell you. Because you're chicken shit, that's why. Hey!"

Travis knocked the bottle from Chuck's hand. It fell, spilling the remaining swigs of beer onto the dusty road where they evaporated within seconds. Chuck moaned and fell to his knees, trying to scoop up the lost beer, but only managing to get his hands dirty. Travis placed his right foot on Chuck's shoulder and shoved, knocking his drunken friend face-first into the dust.

As Chuck struggled to sit up, Travis stared at the house. It was an old Georgian with a narrow porch and dental molding at the roof. It sat atop a high cliff overlooking the Atlantic Ocean. The waves pounded against the shore below, echoing like distant thunder. Two enormous oak trees sat on either side of the house, like two big brothers trying to protect their little sister from the neighborhood bullies.

What had obviously once been magnificent and a grand example of architecture, however, was now nothing more than a hotel for rats. The paint had faded to a ghostly remnant of what it once was. Rotted shingles lay scattered and crumbled around the property. Dead grass and trees, browned and brittle, surrounded the house, as if it had encased the whole area in a glass bubble that let in neither air nor water to nourish their growth.

The only unusual feature, rare for any abandoned home, was that all the windows remained intact. They looked as if they had been painted black from the inside. They were the flat, soulless eyes of a creature that had to watch the world go by, while it withered with age and growing more bitter with each passing day.

Travis sneered down at Chuck, who was still trying to salvage his beer from the dirt, then downed the last swallow of his own. Tossing the bottle onto the ground, he approached the house. As he took his first step onto the dead lawn, the wind whipped out of the east. The two trees rustled their dead limbs and the support columns on the porch sighed. He moved toward the steps and the wind screamed louder, almost knocking him down.

He bent his body forward and scrambled on his hands and feet to get to the porch. As soon as he reached it, the wind died. The whispering trees quieted. Travis looked around, the sudden silence louder than the howling wind of a moment ago. Clearing his throat, he stepped up to the front door and tried to knob. It was locked. He pushed and shoved the weathered wood, but it wouldn't budge.

Now what?

He looked around the porch and saw a lone brick under the window to his right. He picked it up and hefted it in his hand, testing its weight. Looking around at the façade of the house, he couldn't see any sort of obvious masonry. The entire house consisted of wood slats. So where *had* the brick come from? Who would have left it sitting here? Maybe someone planned to break in, but lost their nerve at the last minute.

Grinning, Travis stroked the outside wall of the house with one hand while gripping the brick in the other. He whispered to the structure as if confiding a dark secret to a lifelong friend.

"Well, that's not going to happen tonight, is it? You know I'm coming in, and there's nothing you can do to stop me."

The porch groaned as another gust of wind ripped around the house. The trees leaned in, as if reaching for Travis, encouraging him, wanting him to enter the home. With an almost savage glee, he threw the brick at a first-floor window. The hollow and flat sound of shattering glass barely traveled beyond the dead grass. A stroke of luck, Travis thought, as he smashed out the remaining glass to make a clean entryway into the house.

Grunting as he moved through the opening, Travis side-stepped the brick laying just below the window. He stood with his back to the window and squinted. It was much darker in here than he imagined. He could only discern the vague outlines of several pieces of furniture. Even the streetlight from the corner couldn't penetrate the gloom. He turned to look back out the window, and discovered why the light outside was useless. The window had reformed, as if he'd never broken it. It stared back at him, black as tar, intact.

Travis leaned against the window, feeling around for the seam or handle to open it. Nothing. He scratched at it, still thinking he could remove the paint, but the glass itself was dark and opaque. He pounded his fists against it, willing to risk shredding his own flesh just to get out.

Useless.

He fell to his knees, searching the dark for the brick to smash his way to freedom.

Gone.

Pressing his back against the wall below the window, Travis trembled. "If I ever needed to shit a brick, now would be the time."

Slowly, Travis' eyes adjusted to the gloom. Against the right wall stood a tall block-front desk and chair. Before him sat a dark settee with two high-backed chairs flanking it like soldiers. A long table squatted low in front of the settee and a baby-grand piano huddled in the far corner. The wall on his left opened to a foyer and the stairs to the upper floors lay just beyond the front door.

A dark shape drifted into his peripheral vision and Travis whipped his head toward it. It moved with a slow grace and took on a more defined form as it drew closer. A young girl, pale and thin, stood over him. Her limp brown hair hung in lifeless strands around her face. Her wrinkled cotton shift, simple and grey, draped loosely on her small frame. Her dirty, bare feet bled onto the wooden floor. A dark purple bruise surrounded her throat.

Forever Trapped

Other shapes floated into view behind her: a slender woman in a sweater dress, a stable boy, a set of twin girls dressed in matching frilly, cotton dresses and curls, a tall stately gentleman in top hat and tails, a hunched old woman with ratty hair and missing teeth. Dozens of men and women, boys and girls, in various styles of dress and demeanor, seeped from the woodwork, drifted down from the ceiling, and oozed up through the floor in front of Travis.

Travis' attention was pulled back to the girl standing in front of him. He pushed himself up against the wall, banging his shoulder against the window ledge, but never took his gaze away from her. Her pale blue eyes flicked over him, piercing in their scrutiny. She waved her hand over the assembled group and darkened interior of the house.

"Welcome to my family home."

Travis could only manage a gurgle in response, and the girl sneered. She spun around and faced the gathered crowd. They parted instantly, creating a clear pathway for her to walk. She stepped over to the settee, her feet making dead, hollow slaps with each movement. She motioned over her shoulder for Travis to follow. When he didn't spring into action, the others howled and spun toward him. Screaming, Travis pushed himself off the wall and ran toward the young girl.

Trembling, he stood beside her, keeping a wary eye on the dark shapes that now floated and danced around, moaning in despair. He looked at the pale girl as she sat down, and patted a cushion next to her.

"Sit."

Travis looked from the couch to the girl then to the gathered spirits floating about the room. His legs were locked like rusty hinges and would not bend to allow him to sit as she commanded. The young girl seemed to grow, her body taking new height and width. Her eyes flashed with anger as she roared.

"SIT DOWN!"

Her fury worked better on his rusty knees than any oilcan could have. He fell in fear onto the couch and trembled beside the young girl. She smiled sweetly and stroked his hair. It seemed more of a predatory movement than something to soothe his raw and shaky nerves. Travis thought she wanted him to know that she was in control and at any moment, if the mood struck her, she would gobble him up whole, and pick his boots from her teeth before he felt the first bite.

"That is better," she cooed. "I do not wish for our newest arrival to be ill at ease on his first night of eternity."

Travis shook himself trying to clear the beer from his head. "E-e-eternity?"

"Of course. Those who enter this home never again return to the outside world. You are dead to all those who knew you."

She laughed, a brittle scratching sound that rubbed salt into his raw nerves. "Of course, you are dead to all of us as well."

"I, I don't understand. I'm dead?"

She smirked. "Perhaps not dead-dead. You see, once you stepped upon the withered grass, you passed through the veil between the world of the living and that of the dead. You are neither, yet you are both. You are conscious of yourself and your surroundings, but you have no form or mass except to the other souls here. You feel such powerful emotions, but are powerless to affect the world in any way. All who enter this house find themselves in this same," she paused as she searched for the correct word. "Predicament."

Travis scratched his head in bewilderment. "But I don't understand how-"

The girl shot him a glance that pierced and froze his tongue before he could finish.

"Patience, Travis. All will be revealed to you in time."

She stood, walked past the huddled shapes then through the dark coffee table. Stopping in front of the window through which Travis had entered, she spoke with her back to him. He realized that she was staring not at the street outside but at a remembered vista from her time.

"They built this house for the town elder just before my family arrived. Reverend Brownstone and his wife, Martha, could lord themselves over the entire town from up here. It is easier to keep a man under your boot heel if you stand above him rather than next to him.

"He was judge and jury for the community. He ruled this town according to *his* idea of righteousness and equality. Agree with him and you were pure. Disagree and you were soiled. Doomed was that soul brought before him for trial, for he would surely be found guilty and hanged."

The dozens of dark shapes bobbed and weaved around the young girl as she told her story. They whispered comforts in her ear, caressing her face with their hands. She sighed, entwining her fingers with those of a young boy, as she smiled into his dark eyes.

"My family arrived on a ship in the summertime of 1690. I was fifteen, and so excited about the New World. My papa kept telling me how wonderful it would be to be free from England's chokehold so we could live in peace."

She laughed, a dry sandpaper sound.

"How little he knew."

She turned back to look at Travis, her vision blurry with unspilled tears. She felt the heat of the rage that burned inside her, curling her hands into fists, and shaking them at Travis as if that would help him to understand her suffering. As she walked toward him, the girl spoke. Her voice was cold and flat.

"Within a month, we were branded. My mother, a midwife for the community, helped to birth a baby for the Reverend's sister. It was stillborn. Common it was that many babes, and women, died in childbirth in my time. Nevertheless, the woman would not be consoled. She accused my mother of witchcraft, of killing her baby because my mother could have no more after me."

She fell to her knees in front of Travis. She wept for her mother, for her father, and for herself. Three hundred years had not dulled the pain, but only sharpened its edge, allowing it to cut deeper into the flesh of her memories each time she retold her story.

"My mother denied it, of course. She and my father did everything they could to prove her innocence. But every word, every movement, was twisted against them. People had 'seen' her running naked through the forest on the Sabbath. They saw her talking to the native savages that lived nearby. It was even spoken that she could not have children and so made a pact with the Devil for my life."

Her shoulders slumped as she sat at Travis' feet. She laid her head on his lap, tears spilling onto his jeans, and soaking through the fabric. She struggled to recite the memory of her parents' deaths.

"They came for us late one evening. I was already in bed, and my parents were sitting at the hearth, discussing the problem before them. I heard a great crash as the door was broken down. The Reverend's 'Soldiers for God' burst in, and dragged my parents off to the court. I was taken to the Reverend himself, for if I were a child of Satan, he would be the one to know how best to deal with me.

"I struggled to release myself from their grasp, screaming for my mother, reaching for her receding form as she was hauled off into the darkness for the jail. I struggled so much that the soldiers were forced to drag me the entire way."

She sat up and leaned against the sofa between Travis' knees. She pulled her legs toward her body and traced the torn and bloodied scrapes on the tops of her feet. The wounds still appeared fresh and painful, but she felt no pain when she touched them.

"The Reverend was waiting for me here, in this very room. He had decided my parents were guilty. Not because they were minions of the Devil, but because my mother delivered his stillborn niece. That was all the proof of guilt he required. They were already dead to him, and so I was all that remained of the unholy union between my whore mother and Satan.

"Of course, that did not stop him from…"

She played with the hem of her nightshift. The powerful angry presence she had emanated earlier had evaporated like a wisp of smoke on a strong wind. She was a young girl again, innocent, naïve, and terrified.

"As he saw me as the Devil's spawn, I was nothing and could be treated as such. He sent his wife upstairs to pray for me. When she was gone he," she choked on the memory.

"He forced himself upon me, but in the twisted logic of his mind, he was not soiling himself by bedding me. He was forcing the holiness of God into me through him as a final effort to purify my eternal soul. Or so he claimed."

She stood, and held her hand out to Travis. His attention captured by her story, his face relaxed now with pity instead of taut in fright, he took her offered hand, and followed her as she led him to the window. She pointed to the large oak tree on the left.

"They hanged me from that tree. My hands were bound, as were my feet, so it was no struggle for them to place the noose around my neck. I know God teaches us to love and forgive our enemies, but my heart laid empty. My soul was as black as they believed because they had taken everything from me: my family, my innocence, my faith. And soon, they would have my life.

"I filled that void inside of me with hate. I screamed to the heavens for justice. If I was to die, then all those witness to my destruction would die. My fury anchored my soul to this world and trapped all those who were involved in my death. I cursed anyone who stepped upon this ground to be forever trapped with us."

She squeezed her eyes closed, her sorrow almost unbearable. Then she looked up at Travis and swept a glance over the others.

"I had no idea the power behind my words. I meant only to curse the people of my village who could stand idle and support such actions of these hateful men on behalf of God. And as much as the idea of trapping souls disgusted me, my hate and rage over what was done overshadowed my conscience. Now, I can no longer let go my anger to release us all."

She stood at the window, and Travis imagined she was seeing her body of long ago, twitching and swinging from that oak tree as she died. Tears spilled down her face and Travis could see the spark of hate still burning in her eyes. But he couldn't bring himself to hate her.

Who was he to judge this girl? He was no prince himself. A bully and a petty thief for years, he threatened everyone he encountered into giving him anything and everything he wanted. Shit, he broke into this house with the intent to vandalize it and steal anything he could carry. Sure, his parents were assholes and had just as soon beat the crap out of him as say hello, but he didn't have to be who he was. He didn't have to be the scum of society, living and feeding off the misery and fear of others.

The young boy stepped up to the girl, and wrapped his arm around her waist. He looked up at Travis, and spoke in a thick, cockney accent.

"I keep telling her it ain't her fault. None of us was innocent or pure when we came in here. We prob'ly deserved getting stuck in here forever after the things we done."

He looked sideways at the twin girls. "Well, most of us, anyways."

Travis could feel his brow crinkle as he looked down at the boy.

"What could you have done to deserve getting stuck in here? What are you, like nine years old?"

The boy puffed up his chest in defiance. "I'm eleven, thank you very much. And we'll all tell you our stories. It's the only way we can feel alive again."

The lot of damned souls spoke at once or nodded their heads in agreement. They swarmed around Travis and guided him back to the sofa. As he sat, they gathered near him, but looked to the girl for guidance.

The boy held out his hand. "Tamesin, you must pick."

The young girl smiled, and walked toward the group. She took the boy's hand in both of hers as he guided her to couch next to Travis. She looked at the assembled group as each gazed at her in anticipation. She smiled at the boy.

"Harvey, you speak first. Travis has already asked to hear your story."

The boy sat up straighter and beamed. Tamesin leaned back on the couch, relaxing and motioning for Travis to do the same. As they both settled in, Harvey began his tale.

HARVEY HUDSPETH
(1900)

"We buried my sister this morning."

John Sutton, sitting on a rough slab of rock next to the coal trough, looked over at his friend, Harvey. His brow furrowed.

"Which one?"

Harvey wiped away a tear that had escaped his eye. "Rose, the oldest."

"What happened?"

"Tuberculosis. She was a spinner girl over at Johnson's Textiles. She got sick a few years after she began working there. She'd been coughing on and off for a while, but mother just told her to ignore it and get back to work."

John studied the line of coal lumps as they flew down the chute past them. He picked out a hunk of stone and tossed it to the side. Harvey turned to stare down at the passing coal, but made no move to sort it. John nudged him in the ribs. When Harvey looked up at him, surprised, John jerked his chin in the direction of the foreman.

"If you don't do your job, ol' Black Nose is going to tan your hide. I'm sorry about your sister, Harvey. I really am, but your family might have another funeral this week if you don't get to work."

"We may have one anyway. Samantha has started coughing, too."

John stopped picking debris from the coal. He stared at his friend as Harvey continued.

"She worked over at Johnson's, too. Rose got her the job there. She thought it would be nice to spend time with Samantha, even if it they both ended up half-blind while working at night. Samantha'd been stealing a few bits of thread here and there to make a present for Rose."

Harvey choked on his words. "For her sixteenth birthday. Guess she won't be needing it now."

Another tear streaked down Harvey's face. He could imagine it left a distinct track through the coal dust on his cheek. He smeared it away with the back of his hand. Shaking his head, he leaned forward and began picking through the lumps of coal just as the foreman approached them.

Harvey glanced up as Black Nose walked over. He was aptly nicknamed as years of drinking and bad living had rotted most of the bulbous end of his nose. John continued to work, studying the stream of coal as Black Nose stood over Harvey, scowling.

"What's wrong with you, boy?"

"Nothing, sir."

"'Nothing, sir.' Why don't I believe you?"

He kicked Harvey in the ankle. The boy winced, but continued working. John opened his mouth, but Harvey shook his head to stop him. Nothing John could say or do would deter Black Nose and would only buy John a lashing. The foreman harrumphed and walked away, already turning his unpredictable anger on another unfortunate employee. When he couldn't get a rise out of Harvey, he'd usually find someone else to torture.

The two breaker boys continued working side by side until the ground shook beneath them. They heard men screaming and turned toward the opening of the coal mine. A dozen workers poured out, covered in black and grey dust. Harvey knew that each morning more than a hundred men and boys went into the mines to work. Seeing only a handful exit told him that the rest were either trapped or dead from an explosion and the resulting cave-in.

All the boys and men working outside the mine rushed to its entrance. Each man took an injured or stunned miner on his arm and led him away to safety. Black Nose stood outside the mine entrance and threw his hat to the ground in disgust.

"It'll be hours now before we can get back to work. Dammit all to hell."

Harvey and John moved forward to help the few men stumbling about when Black Nose shouted to them.

"Where the hell do you two think you're going?"

John stammered. "Well, sir, the men need help."

"You'll get some lamps and head in there. The bigger men will move the large rocks, but you two can slip in between and see what's salvageable in there."

"Shouldn't we wait?"

Black Nose towered over the young boy. "Wait? Wait for what?"

"To be sure there are no more cave ins," John answered.

Black Nose shoved John forward then turned to Harvey, but he already had two lamps in hand and nudged his friend toward the mine entrance. They waited behind three brawny men as they moved large chunks of rock and debris from the opening. One of the men, a large burly frowning sort of fellow, fell back, horror painting his face in ashen shock. The other two made signs of the cross and stepped away.

Harvey walked forward and looked down. A small hand lay amidst the rocks, the ragged stump of the wrist still glistened with wet blood. He also saw a black boot, a long leg with the work pant ripped up the side, and a bare arm. Bits of blood and bone and ash covered the ground outside the mine entrance. Harvey bent down and picked up the thin but wiry arm, his finger tracing the long scar down the bicep.

He remembered when that scar first formed, that day at the river when he and his brother spent the afternoon fishing and chasing rabbits. The hook from Harvey's line caught Shinny by surprise as it flew out of the water and scraped down his arm. Instead of getting angry, Shinny growled his best 'argh' and claimed a pirate attack. They splashed and fought for hours until it was time to go home.

Harvey's heart froze solid as he cradled his brother's arm. Shinny had been working down in the mine in spite of his young age. Their mother had faked his birth certificate so Shinny could work in the mine itself, instead of picking through the coal as Harvey did. It was better pay, she had said. John stood next to him, looking over his shoulder. His sharp intake of breath caught everyone's attention around them.

"That. Is that...?" John asked, too shocked to form a complete sentence.

Harvey blinked. "Shinny."

The two large men crossed themselves again as Black Nose stepped up behind Harvey. He grabbed the severed arm from Harvey's hands, and held it up. For a moment, a heavy sadness washed over his features, diminishing their cruel lines. His eyes drooped at the corners and his mouth's hard edge softened. He stared at the assembled group of men. Many of them looked at him in surprise. The foreman was not known for showing any emotion aside from anger.

Black Nose coughed and sputtered. He regained his surly countenance and threw the severed arm at Harvey's feet. He pushed the young boys toward the entrance of the mine, ordered them to find a way in, and look for anything that could be salvaged. Survivors were secondary.

John moved forward, but Harvey stood rooted in place. John looked back at him and Black Nose shoved him again.

"Get your ass moving, boy!"

John reached back and tugged on Harvey's sleeve, but the boy didn't move. Black Nose walked around to face him.

"Did you hear me, you worthless sack of shit? Get in there!"

Harvey lifted his head to stare at the foreman, but made no move to enter the mine. Black Nose leaned forward and breathed a sour rotten puff of air into Harvey's face.

"Just like your brother. Worthless. Even more so now that he's dead."

Harvey frowned. His arm moved before he was even aware of it and he swung the lamp into Black Nose's face. The glass screen shattered, slicing the foreman's flesh. Shards stuck out in a three-dimensional speckled pattern. The dirty oil splattered into the fresh wounds and he howled in pain. The metal frame bruised his cheek and tore into his scalp. Blood poured into Black Nose's eyes and he threw his arms up to protect himself.

Clutching the broken lamp with a firm grip, Harvey arced it back and swung it against Black Nose's raised arm. The foreman fell to his knees and held his arm against his chest, leaving his face vulnerable to another attack. The boy slammed the lamp, or what remained of it, against Black Nose's face again and again, until the metal frame fell to pieces. He then picked up the steel bonnet, and held it high over his head. Black Nose lay stunned on the ground, but his eyes locked onto Harvey. He only had a moment to whimper before the boy slammed the metal dome into his nose, sending shards of bone and cartilage into his brain.

Harvey panted as he stood over the foreman's corpse. Thin lines of blood streaked his face. He looked from one miner to the next, from the burliest of men to the smallest of the boys. They all took a step away from him. His gaze stopped on John. The boy walked over to Harvey, stepping over Black Nose's body, and stood next to his friend. He nodded at him and jutted his chin away, motioning it was time for Harvey to go home. Harvey held out a bloody hand to John and he took it, pumping it several times.

He leaned over Black Nose's body, and spit into the dead man's face. Looking to his right, Harvey stood and spotted the long iron rod used to carry the lanterns through the mines. He picked it up, stepped over the corpse then headed out of the yard. He turned back once to see John waving goodbye. Then his friend and the mine disappeared behind a wall as he turned a corner and headed for home.

As he walked up the steps of the tenement building, his family's life flashed through his memory. Eight people cramped into two rooms; sharing a bathroom with the entire building's occupants; his mother and father fighting non-stop over their poor living conditions and their lack of money. Harvey used to think that if they would stop having children, maybe the money wouldn't be such a problem.

He remembered the day Rose was sent to work. As the oldest child, it was her responsibility to be the first to get a job. When she was nine, she went to work at the textile mill. The rest of the Hudspeth children were too young to work, but Harvey's mother made sure the next in line, Ruby, just seven years old at the time, was at least running errands for the neighbors for a few coins per delivery. With those two employed, Harvey's mother thought they could afford another child. She became pregnant with Samantha, her sixth and last, that spring.

The worn wooden floorboards creaked beneath Harvey's feet as he climbed the four flights of stairs to their apartment. Shinny and William, the two other boys in the family, got jobs as well when they were old enough. Shinny at the mine, and William at the cannery. Harvey was set up at the mine as well, and so Martha and Reginald Hudspeth had their own little supply of ready-made workers to bring in enough money for the family to live on. Harvey's mother and father spent their days counting it and trying to figure out how to spend it: food or booze. The latter won more often than the former. As their children slaved, the parents reaped the benefits.

His hand on the door, Harvey could hear Samantha coughing from inside the apartment. There was a loud crash as his mother threw something against the wall, her voice screeching above it.

"God dammit, Samantha. Can't you stop coughing for one second? My head is killing me and you're not helping one bit!"

Harvey sneered, thinking if she weren't recovering from her latest bender, then her head wouldn't hurt so much. He pushed open the door to find his mother lying on the couch to his right, her hands gripping the sides of her head. The glass she had thrown laid in pieces on the floor across the room. Samantha sat in the corner, curled into a ball, crying, and still coughing.

Harvey ran to Samantha's side. A trickle of blood ran down her cheek from a small cut above her right eye. He wiped the blood away and pulled her into his arms.

"Sshhh. It's all right, Samantha. I'm here now. I'm here."

"Oh, will you two please *shut up*!?" his mother yelled.

Harvey disengaged himself from his little sister and led her into the bedroom. He told her to lay down and take a nap. She didn't need to go to work today. He looked up and saw Ruby, the second oldest girl, sitting in the corner on a dirty blanket, reading a torn and ragged book. Her hands were gnarled and deformed from an accident at one of the spinning machines at Johnson's three years ago when she was eleven. She couldn't work and so was left to her own devices each day, neither his mother nor his father caring what she did.

He motioned her over to the bed to lie with Samantha.

"Ruby, will you watch over Samantha? I need to talk to mother for a moment."

Ruby looked at the long metal rod in Harvey's hand. She opened her mouth, but he stopped her.

"Just stay in here, all right? Don't come out until I tell you to. Can you do that?"

She nodded, and crawled under the covers with Samantha. She wrapped her arms around the younger girl and hummed an old lullaby to help her fall asleep. Harvey nodded, smiling, and walked back out into the main room, closing the bedroom door behind him. His mother was still on the couch, her fingers rubbing small circles against her temples to soothe her headache. He dragged the metal pole behind him as he approached her. She frowned and looked up, glaring at him.

"For Christ's sake, Harvey. What are you trying to do, kill me with all that racket?"

"Shinny's dead."

She continued to rub her temples and squeezed her eyes shut. "What?"

"I said, Shinny's dead, mother."

Her eyes snapped open. She turned her head to look at Harvey, disbelief clouding her eyes.

"What? What happened?"

"There was an explosion. Shinny was in the mine when it happened."

Tears welled up in her eyes. She rubbed a hand across her face. Her voice was strained with despair.

"How in the name of God are we supposed to live now? Shinny's earnings were keeping this family afloat."

Harvey squinted as his forehead furrowed in anger. His knuckles burned white as he clenched the metal rod in his hands with all his might. He raised it above his head and held it there, pausing as the last bit of love he ever felt for this woman evaporated from his heart. She continued to sob on the couch, her hands covering her eyes. She never saw the rod as it slammed into the side of her face.

A little while later, he opened the bedroom door. He could still hear Ruby humming from underneath the covers. He leaned the rod against the wall and reached over to tug on the blanket. Ruby peeked out from beneath it. She studied Harvey, and the blood that soaked his shirt and covered his face and hands. Her eyes widened.

"Are you all right, Harvey?"

"Yes, Ruby. I'm fine. It's not my blood."

She swallowed. "Momma?"

He nodded. Ruby gave a half smile as she breathed out a sigh of relief. Her smile faded, though, almost as soon as it curled her lips. She looked out the bedroom door.

"What about Papa?"

"Don't you worry about him. I want you and Samantha to go downstairs and stay with Mrs. Flannaghan, all right?"

She nodded and nudged Samantha, who had fallen into a fitful sleep between coughs. The younger girl rubbed her eyes and asked what was going on. Ruby shushed her then gave Samantha her favorite doll. Ruby took her book in one hand, her sister in the other, and moved to leave. Harvey jumped in front of both of them, standing between them and the sight of their mother's body. He ushered them through the living room, holding his hands over their eyes, until they reached the door.

Harvey hurried them out into the hallway and toward the stairs.

"I'll come get you when it's time. Just watch over Samantha, and be good for Mrs. Flannaghan."

He bent down and kissed Samantha on the top of her head. Standing, he looked at Ruby. Her blue eyes were dark behind unspilled tears. She brushed a hand across his cheek and nodded. She grabbed Samantha's hand and pulled her down the stairs. Harvey turned back and entered their apartment. He sat on the floor opposite the door and waited for his father.

Hours later, long after the sun had sunk below the horizon and the sight of his mother's stiffened corpse no longer made him shiver, Harvey's ears pricked up as the floor outside the door groaned. His father had finally shuffled home after his usual trip to the saloon to spend what little money they had left that month. A loud thump sounded against the door, most likely his father fumbling to get the door open and slamming his head against the wood. The angry curse that followed confirmed Harvey's assumption.

Still sitting on the floor, Harvey propped up the long iron rod in front of him, leaning forward and resting his head against it. He didn't look up as his father entered, nor did he make any indication that he was there, waiting. His father stumbled against Harvey's legs. He leaned down and squinted.

"Wha, what's going on?"

As with Black Nose, before he realized what he was doing, Harvey grabbed the rod and swiped it behind his father's knees, knocking the drunken man to the floor. The air whooshed out of his lungs as he landed. Coughing, he struggled to catch his breath. Giving him no time, Harvey raised the rod and slammed it into his father's chest. He did it several more times to make sure his father was sufficiently hurt to keep the fight out of him.

Harvey walked to the cupboard against the far wall and pulled out a candle and matches. Electricity was too expensive for them to have, even without his parents' financial irresponsibility. He placed the candle on the floor next to his father's head. The older man struggled to breathe, so Harvey spoke loud enough for him to hear.

"I need to tell you three things, Father. One…"

Harvey pulled a match from the small box and lit it.

"Mother is dead."

His father's coughing paused for a moment. When he resumed, Harvey touched the flame to the candlewick.

"Two, Shinny is dead, which brings the count of dead children to three. First Rose, then William, now Shinny. Bad luck, old man, wouldn't you say?"

The candle now lit, Harvey picked it up and held it closer to his face. His mother's blood painted his cheeks in brown stains. The white shirt he wore was now rust-colored and stiff with dried blood. He pushed his face forward and his father shrunk away.

"Three, you're dead, too."

His father managed to scream once before Harvey slammed the iron rod into his skull. Despite already killing the foreman and his mother earlier today, Harvey was overflowing with energy, fueled by rage, disappointment, sorrow, and hatred. His eleven-year old body channeled the strength of all the children forced into labor to support their families. Rose, his oldest sister, dead from tuberculosis brought on by breathing in the dust and particles floating around the textile mill every day; William, his second older brother, killed after falling into one of the machines at the cannery; and now Shinny, blown to pieces in a mine explosion.

His siblings, his neighbors, his friends, his fellow workers. Perhaps all of their souls were working through him to satisfy their need for vengeance. Whatever the source, Harvey welcomed it, using it to swing the rod over and over again, crushing his father's head into a crimson pulp. When he finished, he let the rod slip from his fingers and clang to the floor. He fell to his knees and wept.

Thirty minutes later, Harvey had cleaned his face and hands, changed into fresh clothes, and carried a small satchel filled with what few belongings he had: the rest of the food in the house and a handful of dollars he found hidden in his parents' dresser. He hurried down the stairs and stood outside Mrs. Flannaghan's apartment door. He raised his hand to knock, but stopped.

He needed to leave town as soon as possible and he couldn't take his sisters with him. Seeing them now would make it that much harder to leave. Mrs. Flannaghan and her husband were childless and would take great care of Ruby and Samantha. His best, and only, option was to leave now and never turn back. He laid his hand on the door, wished them a silent goodbye, then darted out the front entrance of the building.

He ran through back alleys and darkened streets until he reached the train yard. Seeing an open car, he hopped into it and pushed himself into the corner, hiding as best he could from the railroad bulls. His timing had been perfect. Within minutes, the train jerked into motion and was soon streaming across the countryside.

Within hours he was miles from him home. The landscape changed, but the same stars shone in the night sky. He fell asleep counting them and thinking of his dead siblings. He snapped awake just as the train came to a stop, the pale glow on the horizon indicating a new day. Harvey quickly gathered his belongings, and leaped out from the train car. He made a dash for the dense woods off to his right, succeeding in avoiding notice or capture. Shinny once told him that anyone caught riding the train without paying was thrown in jail and tortured to death with boiling water and ice tongs. Harvey didn't know if that was true, but he sure wasn't going to find out.

After an hour of walking, Harvey came to the edge of the woods. It opened on a dirt road. To his left he could just make out a few small buildings and could hear the rustle of the busy midday crowd of whatever town laid down there. To his right, the dirt road continued straight and crested over a hill in the distance. Harvey followed the road away from town, hoping to find a place to hide during the day before continuing his travels through the cover of night.

To his left, a large home perched at the top of the hill. As he neared it, he noticed the overgrown weeds and large dead trees in the front yard. It seemed obvious that no one lived here and that was perfect for Harvey. He walked around the side of the home and noted the cliff at the back of the property. Sauntering over to it, he tried to look casual, but swiveled his head left and right scanning for anyone else who might be in the area. He looked up at the back of the house, but all the windows were dark and he couldn't see any movement inside.

Standing at the edge of the cliff, he looked down. The waves crashed against black jagged rocks and echoed like thunder. Despite the growing heat of the morning, goose bumps prickled Harvey's skin, and he stepped away from the edge. He'd better get inside before anyone happened by.

He jogged back to the front, stopping to hide against the worn wood of the house as he checked the empty yard. Nothing. With a quick hop he was on the porch. Passing the front window, he thought it odd that he couldn't see anything past the black glass. Maybe the previous owners had painted over them, though for what reason he couldn't imagine.

He stood at the screen door and knocked, a polite habit he wasn't quite ready to shake off. He called out.

"Hello? Anyone home?"

He knocked again and still only the silence greeted him. Harvey smiled to himself as he pulled open the screen and tried the knob of the front door. It turned easily. With one last look around, he slipped though the entryway and pushed the door closed behind him. In seconds, whispers tickled his ears. His eyes struggled to adjust to the gloomy interior. Dark shadows floated around him. They seemed to be coming out of the walls, the floor, even the gloom itself.

At last, one form took shape amongst the shadows. A young girl, not much older than Harvey, pushed through the darkness and stood before him. Her voice soothed his raw nerves and tired soul.

"Welcome, Harvey. You're home now."

She reached out a hand, and caressed his cheek.

SEBASTIAN BULLOCK
(MODERN DAY)

He plucked at his twelve-string guitar, rolling the final chord of the song on his fingertips. His steel blue eyes locked on a young man in the front row who looked like he couldn't be more than eighteen years old. Sebastian smiled, flashing his straight white teeth in an almost predatory fashion. The guy actually blushed. Even in the dim light of the club, Sebastian could see his cheeks flush with color.

As the young man studied his fingers, Sebastian looked to the back of the room to catch his wife's attention. A slim, blonde woman raised her chin to acknowledge him. Sebastian nodded toward the patron in the front and the woman nodded in return. She wove her way through the crowd and sat down next to the young man. After a few minutes of whispering in his ear and gesturing toward Sebastian, the man nodded. They both rose from the table and headed backstage. The woman winked at Sebastian as she and the man disappeared behind a small door.

After playing one final song for the set, Sebastian stood and thanked the crowd for coming.

"Please hang around for a little while longer, won't you? Up next is a brilliant young guitarist, William James. I'm sure he will entertain you even more than I have."

The crowd applauded as he walked off-stage. He gave one last smile and wave before he followed his wife behind the stage door. She looked up as he entered, but he put a finger to his lips. She was sitting on a small couch just beside the doorway with the man, who had his back to Sebastian. She smiled and looked back to their guest then ran her fingers through his wavy hair and gave a soft laugh. Sebastian slammed the door and the man jumped and turned his head, embarrassment coloring his cheeks.

"Well, well, well. What have we here? My wife and…?"

He bent forward as he leaned his guitar against the couch. He raised his eyebrows as he waited for an answer. The man coughed, but Sebastian's wife spoke instead while she twirled her fingers in the man's hair.

"Sebastian, this is Tony. Tony, this is my husband, Sebastian."

Tony stood, rubbing his hands on his jeans before reaching one out to Sebastian. Sebastian stared at Tony's hand for a moment, hoping to make him feel uneasy. Once he felt he had succeeded, he firmly gripped it, and pumped it twice.

"Nice to meet you, Tony. So, did you like my show?"

The man nodded. "Oh, yeah. It was great. I mean, yeah, it was really great."

Sebastian's mouth curled up into a sly grin as his wife, Marilyn, got up from the couch. Tony had no idea she had ever moved, let alone stood inches from his back. Sebastian smoothed a hand over Tony's chest and the young man sighed and closed his eyes. As he did so, Sebastian winked at

Marilyn, letting her know that she could have the fun with this quarry tonight, after he was finished with the guy, of course. Smiling, she slipped her hands into the front pockets of Tony's jeans. Tony jumped in surprise. Sebastian whispered.

"Sshhh. Now don't be nervous, Tony. It's all right if my wife joins in the fun, isn't it?"

"Uh, sure, I guess."

Marilyn wiggled her hands in Tony's pockets and gently squeezed the young man's genitals. Sebastian moved forward and put one hand between Tony's legs. With the other, he grabbed his wife's hair, pulling her close for a hard kiss. Between them Tony moaned in pleasure.

Later, as the three of them lay in bed, Tony between Sebastian and Marilyn, they shared a fat joint. Tony closed his eyes and took a deep draw. Sebastian nodded to his wife as he slipped out from beneath the red silk sheets. Tony's eyes snapped open as he felt the shift in weight on the bed. He looked up at Sebastian, his eyes soft and moist like a helpless puppy.

"Where are you going?"

"Just heading to the bathroom. Don't look so sad, Tony. I'm coming right back."

Naked, Sebastian made his way to the bathroom, taking one look over his shoulder at his wife. She leaned over her side of the bed. Slipping her hand between the mattress and box spring, she pulled out a wicked, eight-inch steel blade. She held it up so only Sebastian could see it, then licked its edge as she gripped the dragon-shaped hilt. Sebastian smiled, and closed the door behind him.

He rolled another joint in the bathroom. Sitting on the edge of the bathtub, he sparked the reefer and closed his eyes as he listened to the screams coming from the bedroom. The first were screams of surprise. Those were the most amusing. To hear the absolute shock in someone's voice as Marilyn, or himself, stopped being amorous, and turned the evening into a deadly dance, never failed to entertain him.

The next screams held fear and pain. Those always got him hard. He laid back in the tub and masturbated, his hand speeding up or slowing down, depending on the volume and frequency of the shrieks in the bedroom. He came, as usual, when the shouts turned to gagging, and the victim choked on his own blood.

After cleaning himself up in the sink, he exited the bathroom. Marilyn lay on her back on the bed, bright red blood coating her from head to toe. Her blonde hair clung to her neck and shoulders. Crimson streaks painted her bare skin. She arched upwards as she licked the blood from her fingers, drawing them down her cheeks, to her lips, and along her neck. She turned her head to watch Sebastian's approach, and she held a hand out to him.

He took it and slid into bed. Turning toward Sebastian, she pushed Tony's body to the edge of the mattress with her foot. His corpse rolled onto its side and faced them. Marilyn pulled Sebastian on top of her and clamped her lips onto his. He moaned into her mouth as she ground her hips against him. As he entered her, Sebastian turned to look at Tony's empty eyes. Even in death, Tony appeared terrified, and in agony. Sebastian came within minutes.

As they wrapped the body and bed sheets in plastic, Sebastian poked Tony's corpse.

"So, where are we going to dump this one?"

"Well, I was scouting around the town when we first got here. Nothing around here is suitable. But on the outskirts, near the cliffs, there're a lot of empty lots, and a few abandoned houses. We could toss it into the sea without anyone ever finding out."

"Brilliant. I knew there was a reason I married you, besides your great ass."

In the darkest hour of the night, Sebastian and Marilyn snuck the plastic bundle to their car. After tossing it into the trunk, they retrieved what little luggage they had from their room and placed it in the back seat. Marilyn drove the car out of town toward the place she thought would be great to dump the body.

She pulled the car into a rough driveway and followed it around to the back of an abandoned home. The cliffs were a hundred yards beyond the edge of the property. She parked the car and turned off the engine. Sebastian glanced back at the large empty home.

"Are you sure it's abandoned?"

"Pretty sure. Wanna take a peek, just in case?"

"I think we'd better. If we find anyone, we'll have them catch a ride with Tony."

They walked hand in hand around to the front, scanning what little they could see of the yard. Nothing moved or made any noise. In fact, all sound seemed to have been muffled as if a giant plastic bubble covered the house. They made their way up the worn front steps, Marilyn clinging to Sebastian in fear, the first he'd ever seen her express since he'd known her. When they approached the front door, Sebastian pounded on it and called out.

"Hello?"

When no one answered, he tried it again. When he was met with silence a second time, he pulled open the screen and turned the doorknob. The front door opened.

"Sebastian," Marilyn squeaked in his ear.

"It's all right, hon. We've got to do this. Don't worry. I won't let anything happen to you."

They stepped into the dark foyer. Again Sebastian called out.

"Hello?"

Dark shadowy figures appeared from the walls, the floor, and the ceiling. They swirled around Sebastian and Marilyn, all speaking, crying, and moaning at once. Just as it was becoming unbearable, it stopped, and one strong commanding voice floated over them.

"Let us all give our new friends a warm welcome."

The front door slammed shut behind them.

MR. COPPERWELL
(1923)

Mr. Copperwell slipped one hundred dollars to the doorman as he escorted his newest niece into the lobby of the hotel. Pressing a gloved finger to his lips, he winked at the lone late-evening employee, who slid his eyes away as he pocketed the money.

Coppy, as his friends called him, stroked the long mahogany curls on Helen's head, careful not to muss the perfect ringlets. There would be time enough for that later on. But for now he must present his perfect manners and beautiful guest with all the shine he could muster. No one, outside his hotel room walls, need know about his fetish fantasies and dirty little secrets.

Helen's shoes tapped along the marble lobby floor, keeping in time with the swish-swish rhythm of her white lace frock. Mr. Copperwell studied her from behind as she walked ahead of him toward the elevator. She was thin and rather narrow, but her hips rounded just enough on either side to capture his interest and hold it. His pulse quickened with lust and the promise of pain to come. He allowed her to push the button to call the elevator, giving her a sense of control, however fleeting or false it may be. Coppy extended his arm forward as the doors opened, brandishing his chivalry for good effect.

Coppy led the young lady to his suite. Once inside, he pointed toward a purple and maroon colored sofa where she could sit down. He leaned his back against the door as it closed, blocking his movements as he twisted the lock into place with a soft *snick*. After slipping off his overcoat, he laid it, his hat, and cane on the sideboard near the door.

He walked into the living room and Helen watched him, smiling, as he picked up a covered plate from the coffee table. With a flourish, he pulled away the cover to reveal a selection of chocolates. Helen almost squealed with delight.

"Chocolates! My favorite. How did you know?"

"Oh, I have spies everywhere, my dear. They tell me all sorts of things. Now, please try one."

Helen held her hand over the plate, waving it back and forth as she tried to decide which piece to take. She decided on a large round delight and placed the whole piece in her mouth. Her cheek bulged with the strain of the large confection, but she managed to work it down quickly.

Mr. Copperwell smiled.

"Wonderful. Do have another, my dear."

Helen's eyes widened.

"Really?"

"Of course. You may have as many as you like."

Helen snatched two more pieces. One she popped into her mouth. The other she held in her hand until she could make room for it. When finished, she licked melted chocolate from each of her delicate fingers, an act that threw Mr. Copperwell into a sexual frenzy. He set the plate in front of her then straightened, licking his lips. He stepped around the table. She sat motionless with her thumb in her mouth, the melted chocolate forgotten as his imposing figure loomed over her. He lowered himself to the sofa next to her.

He pulled her hand away from her face; her thumb remained smudged with traces of chocolate. He stared at it as he spoke.

"You know I like you, yes?"

Helen nodded as her cheeks blushed a soft pink.

"And I know I'm a bit older than you. But as your elder, I want you to trust me. Can you do that, Helen?"

Again she nodded. He smiled and pulled her hand toward his mouth. She gasped as he sucked the remaining chocolate from her tiny digit. For the first time that evening, she felt afraid. He could see it in her eyes. She tried to pull her hand away, but he squeezed, refusing to release it.

Helen cried out, or at least she tried. It came out as more of a whimper instead. Her lungs refused to fill with enough air to create a scream. She blinked while struggling to keep her eyes open. He guessed the sedative soaked sweets had begun to shut down her defenses. She sagged back against the sofa as her muscles relaxed. Her eyelids lowered against her will, but not enough to block out the sight of Coppy biting into her soft flesh and tearing her thumb away from her hand.

He smiled. He could feel her blood covering his lips and teeth. Before she fell into blackness, Coppy laughed.

The following morning, Mr. Copperwell sauntered into the hotel restaurant. The soft lines of his sack suit flowed with each step, his movements as smooth as fresh cream. He pulled out his silver pocket watch, still sparkling in its newness, calmly noting the hour. His relaxed demeanor never belied the rush from his enthusiastic participation in the horrific activities of the previous evening.

He took his usual table near the window. With a quick nod to a passing waiter, he was served coffee and a breakfast menu. Mr. Copperwell always had a voracious appetite the morning after a good session. After he ordered eggs, bacon, toast, juice, and pancakes with extra syrup, he sipped his coffee as he gazed out at the bustling city street.

Just then he overheard a distraught woman speaking to the manager of the restaurant. He felt his eyes widen as he focused on the conversation.

"Please, you must help me," the woman begged. "She's been missing since last night. Are you sure you haven't seen anyone fitting her description?"

"I'm sorry, madam, but I did not see her. Even if I couldn't remember her face, I'm sure I would remember if a twelve-year-old girl came through here yesterday."

"But–"

"Please, feel free to speak with any of the employees. Or perhaps one of our guests saw her."

The woman nodded her head, biting her lower lip, as she scanned the restaurant. She smoothed her hands over her rumpled dress, aware of her shabby appearance despite the trauma of her missing daughter. She caught Mr. Copperwell's stare and took a tentative step in his direction. When he smiled, she straightened her stance and strode toward him.

"I'm sorry to bother you, sir, but maybe you can help me."

"My dear woman. I couldn't help but overhear your conversation with Mr. Nicholas. You said your daughter is missing?"

"Yes," she cried. "She went to a party with her aunt and uncle, my husband's brother and his wife, last night at The Grand. But come ten o'clock, they couldn't find her. Please, can you help me?"

"What does she look like?"

"Well, she's twelve years old. Long dark brown hair. She had it curled in wide ringlets specially for the party. She was wearing a white lace dress."

Mr. Copperwell stroked his chin as he processed her information. He squinted.

"Was she rather on the thin side, about this tall?" He held his hand level with the woman's shoulder.

"Yes! Lord in heaven, have you seen her?"

"I believe I have. As I was walking toward the hotel's main entrance last night, I saw a young girl, fitting your daughter's description, walking down the sidewalk with a young man. He looked to be around thirty or so and she was smiling and laughing with him. I assumed they were related, like uncle and niece, so I thought nothing more of it and entered the hotel."

The haggard faced woman paled as if all the blood in her body had just drained out through her feet. Her body sagged and Mr. Copperwell lurched to grab her before she fell to the floor. A small secret smile tugged at his lips, but he tucked it away as soon at is had appeared. He called for the host.

"Mr. Nicholas! Call a doctor and the police while you're at it."

Several hours later, the woman, Mrs. Darcy, was resting back in her home and Mr. Copperwell wrapped up his interview with the police at the hotel. He gave them all the information he could "remember" about the little girl, Helen, and the man who was now believed to be her kidnapper. He would never forgive himself for letting them slip away. But how was he to know? The constable assured him it wasn't his fault and tried to convince Mr. Copperwell that this new information could possibly save the little girl's life. He supposed the constable was right and Coppy thanked him for his understanding, and if there was anything else the police needed, he'd be happy to help.

As the constable excused himself and turned to leave, Mr. Copperwell smirked at his back. How many police officers had he given the run-around with that old story? Too many to count. He took the last sip of his coffee, cold and bitter now, then waved farewell to Mr. Nicholas.

The following weekend, Mr. Copperwell sat at another linen covered table at yet another stale and boring "social event of the year" with the same stiff and dry crowd that seemed to come pre-packaged for just such occasions. What he wouldn't give for some excitement, *his* kind, to liven things up a bit. He had to be careful, though. Helen entertained him only a week prior. He could still feel her soft curls under his fingers, hear her muffled grunts through the gag, and taste her sweet blood on his tongue. His arousal grew just thinking of her, and the itch to feel another small body as it struggled helplessly against him began to tickle his skin, his muscles, and his soul. It needed scratching.

He shook his head. He had to push these thoughts away. It was too soon for another treat. But just as he steeled his will, temptation walked through the door.

A young couple in their thirties stepped into the room, trailed by two tow-headed young girls. Twins. Mr. Copperwell could hardly take his eyes off them. Each girl had glossy short hair parted on the side with shiny, pink satin bows pinned on the left above the ear. Ice blue eyes scanned the room, not with fear or shyness, but with an eagerness not common in children when they find themselves in a room full of strangers. Their pink satin dresses shone in the chandelier light and white patent leather shoes completed their outfits.

Mr. Copperwell saw one of his oldest business associates, Mr. Morse, sidle up to the couple and begin talking. Copperwell couldn't pass up this chance and leaped to his feet, then weaseled into the conversation.

"Morse, old man. You must introduce me to this charming young couple."

"Ah, Coppy. Of course. Mr. Copperwell, may I introduce Donald Andrews, son of Armstrong Andrews."

"As in Andrews' Construction, Andrews' Consolidated?"

Morse nodded. "The very same. His lovely wife, Veronica. And their beautiful little girls, Emmaline and Evangeline."

Mr. Copperwell shook Donald's hand, and kissed Veronica's, after each was offered.

"Pleasure to meet you both." He bent down to be eye to eye with the twins. "A pleasure to meet all of you, especially such beautiful young ladies as yourselves."

The girls giggled and curtseyed. Mr. Copperwell almost fainted in delight. He stood again to face Donald and Veronica.

"How charming they are. How old are they?"

"They just turned ten last week," Veronica smiled.

Copperwell smiled down at the girls. "My goodness. Ten years old already? I suppose then that you're too sophisticated and grown up for candy."

"No! We love candy!" the girls cried in unison.

"Is that so? Well, with your parents' permission, I would be happy to direct you both to a table on the far side of the room that is absolutely smothered with all kinds of sweets."

"May we have some candy, Mother?" Evangeline tugged at her mother's arm.

"Please?" Emmaline begged as well.

"Well, we are at a party. I suppose it would be all right. Thank you, Mr. Copperwell."

"Not at all. Now, young ladies. Please come with me."

He held out both his hands and took each girl in tow. The soft silk of their skin caused him to shudder in delight as he led them to the dessert table. If he played his cards right, they would be dessert for him very soon.

Four days later, Mr. Copperwell got his wish. As he strolled down the street one Wednesday afternoon, he saw Mrs. Andrews and the twins walking ahead of him. Mrs. Andrews struggled with a large hat box, several overloaded bags, and her daughters, who were trying to steer her into a toy shop by pulling at her arms. As she juggled the packages and resisted the constant grabbing of her girls, the box tumbled from her grasp and crashed to the sidewalk, spilling an ornate feathered and silk cloche hat into a large puddle.

The twins immediately let go of their mother and took several steps away from her. Mrs. Andrews appeared as if she might faint. Mr. Copperwell rushed to her side to lend his support.

"Mrs. Andrews, are you all right?"

"My, my," she stammered.

He glanced down at the hat, and tsked quietly.

"Oh, my goodness. What a shame. Surely all is not lost, though."

He stooped down and picked up the sodden hat between his thumb and forefinger. He twisted it back and forth.

"Well, ahem. At least the water was clean. I'm sure if you just let it dry out, it will be fine. I suppose."

He grabbed the box, and placed the soaking headpiece inside. Mrs. Andrews looked lost as she stared at the dripping mess laying in the bottom of the box. Mr. Copperwell guided her to a nearby bench, and forced her to sit down. Evangeline and Emmaline, holding hands, approached their mother. Tears welled in their eyes as they whispered an apology.

"We're sorry, Mother. We didn't mean to."

Mrs. Andrews' brow furrowed in anger. She opened her mouth to reprimand the young girls, but Mr. Copperwell interrupted.

"Now, Mrs. Andrews. I'm sure the girls really didn't mean any harm. That said, however, you look like you could use some pampering. Allow me to call my driver. He can be here in just a few minutes to take you home, to get something to eat, whatever you'd like. He will be at your disposal for the afternoon. I would be more than happy to watch the girls for you. I happen to know of a wonderful soda shop just around the corner."

Veronica Andrews' face lost its hard edge. A grateful smile curled her lips, and she nodded. Mr. Copperwell ducked into Harwell's drug store to use the phone to call his driver. Just as he left the store, he overheard Mrs. Andrews instructing the girls. She pulled her daughters close.

"Would you like to spend the day with Mr. Copperwell?"

The girls nodded, their blonde bobbed hair bouncing in unison.

"All right. Don't let him fill you up with too many sweets. We're having dinner at Mr. Morse's house tonight. And remember your manners. Say 'please' and 'thank you', understand?"

"Yes, Mother."

"Good."

Coppy smiled, imagining *he* would have the twins for dinner someday soon.

Five minutes later, Mr. Copperwell hefted the shopping bags into the front seat of his car then helped Mrs. Andrews into the back. He leaned in through the front window to instruct Phillip to take Mrs. Andrews wherever she wanted to go. He would be home later that afternoon.

When the car pulled away, Coppy and the two girls waved good-bye as it drove down the street. The three of them

Forever Trapped

walked hand in hand down the sidewalk, away from the receding automobile.

"So, ladies. Where should we go first? The soda shop, the candy parlor, or the toy store?"

The girls squealed in unison. "Candy!"

"Wonderful," he purred.

An hour later, Mr. Copperwell and the girls walked toward the edge of town. He knew of an abandoned house where he could spirit the girls away. Not that he was going to harm them, or do anything else. Yet. But he needed to solidify their trust in him. If he could make them feel safe and protected in a spooky old house, then he just might get their gratitude for life, however long that might be.

"Say, how would you girls like to go on an adventure?"

Their eyes widened. "What do you mean, like on a pirate ship?" Evangeline asked.

"Or a treasure hunt?" Emmaline asked.

"Tush, nothing so mundane. I'm talking about a haunted house!"

Emmaline's mouth dropped in fear. And though Evangeline gaped the same way, her eyes shone with a fevered curiosity. Mr. Copperwell had learned earlier that Evangeline was the more adventurous of the twins, so he played to that side of her, hoping she would help him convince Emmaline to take the chance.

"I can't honestly say it *is* haunted. I've never been inside, but that's the story everyone else in town has told me. What do you say? Shall we take a look?"

Evangeline nodded, but Emmaline shook her head.

"I don't want to see a ghost."

"Emmie, Mr. Copperwell just said there was no proof of ghosts. I'm sure it's just a story people tell each other so they don't sound as dull as they really are."

Mr. Copperwell covered a smile behind his hand. Evangeline was very bright for her age. Such a feisty little personality. She'll be a great treat to enjoy later. He'd have to think of something special just for her.

"You wouldn't let a ghost get me, would you, Vange? I mean, if there were any."

"Of course not. I'll never let anything bad happen to you," Evangeline assured her sister by grabbing her hand. "Besides, Mr. Copperwell will be there to protect us both, right Mr. Copperwell?"

"Of course, my dears. I wouldn't dream of letting anyone else get to you. And please, call me Coppy."

A mile outside of town, Mr. Copperwell was carrying Emmaline as Evangeline skipped ahead, picking wildflowers along the way. Emmaline rested her head on his shoulder and wrapped both arms around his neck. She had become so at ease with him that she had forgotten her earlier fear at the possibility of seeing a ghost.

As they crested a hill, a giant old Georgian style house loomed ahead of them. Mr. Copperwell could see the edge of a cliff behind the house and heard the roar of waves crashing against the shore below. Evangeline stopped in her tracks and waited for Mr. Copperwell and her sister to catch up. She immediately grabbed his hand as he stood next to her. Her bravado had retreated in the face of the bleak and darkened home.

"Are you sure it's safe?"

"Of course. It's just an old house. It only looks scary on the outside. I don't even believe in ghosts, do you, my dear?"

"Well, I guess not."

"What about you, Emma? You're not afraid, are you?"

Emmaline chewed on her bottom lip as she studied the house. It frightened her, but she probably didn't want to admit it if her sister and Coppy weren't scared.

"N-n-no."

Mr. Copperwell smiled and thrust his chin toward the house.

"Then let's press on, shall we?"

He gently lowered Emmaline to the ground and took her hand. Guiding both girls up the front walk, he became lost in his thoughts of how he might get the twins back here when the time was right and what he would do to them. A gentle tug on his sleeve brought him out of his reverie.

"Hmm, yes? What is it, Evangeline?"

"Why is the grass all brown?"

Mr. Copperwell scanned the yard around them. Indeed, the grass was brown and dried. A large section of the lawn was dead, as were the large oak trees on either side of the walkway. Their gnarled limbs and black bark looked like charred skeletal hands reaching up from a long dead fire pit. He shivered as a cold breeze swirled around them.

"Well, my dear. As the house is abandoned, there's no one to take care of the grounds. Naturally, all the grass would be dead."

As they ascended the steps, he was able to shake the uneasy feeling in his belly as he thought about the adventures they could have inside the house, all alone, with no one around for miles to interrupt them.

"Here we are, ladies. Are you ready for the big adventure?"

Emmaline and Evangeline nodded their heads despite their obvious fear. They grasped Mr. Copperwell's hands tighter as he pushed open the front door and they crossed the threshold together. As their eyes adjusted to the gloom, the door slammed closed, locking them away from the outside world, and into Tamesin's welcoming arms. Forever.

DANIEL WEAVER
(1984)

Holding a rolled dollar bill inside his left nostril, Daniel inhaled a line of cocaine from his pocket mirror. He repeated the ritual on the right side. He leaned back against the tile wall of the bathroom stall, the toilet flushing mechanism jammed into his back. Straightening again, he made sure not to dip any part of his suit in the toilet water. Instead, he tilted his head backwards and took a few quick snorts of air to force the drug all the way into his nasal cavity.

Daniel wiped the mirror clean with his forefinger and rubbed the small remnants of coke onto his gums before pocketing the mirror and the rolled bill. He smoothed down his tie and jacket as he exited the stall.

The bathroom was empty, so he took his time fidgeting with his hair. He wiped a smudge of white powder off the tip of his nose and took a few cursory sniffs. With one last tweak on a stray lock of hair, he winked at his reflection and headed back to his office.

Daniel Weaver was the Public Relations Director of the Jackson, White, and Torrance advertising agency. And though he was a brilliant PR man, he had a bit of a drug problem. Maybe a slight dependency on alcohol as well. Definitely an addiction to murder. Not that anyone knew about any of his little issues. As long as he made the clients happy and didn't steal from the company, he was the perfect employee. And he'd stop anyone who tried to say differently.

In fact, he already had. More than once. He couldn't remember the exact number of people he'd killed so far. That coke was a real brain scrambler. Maybe he should cut back a bit. It wouldn't help his career to forget that he had stuffed a corpse in his closet just as he opened it to hang up the boss' coat.

His most recent kill had been a hoot, though. Some brown-nosing sycophant caught him snorting blow at the Christmas party last week. What was the guy's name? Gerald. Or was it Jim? Didn't matter now. The little prick tried to blackmail Daniel. So under the pretense of a secret meeting to pay him off, Daniel ambushed Johnny-boy in the darkness of an abandoned parking garage. It turned out that ramming a steel spike into the ass-kisser's skull was much easier than he first thought. Not quite like a hot knife through warm butter, but more like a warm spoon into a tub of cold margarine.

He had snuck up behind the little turd so when the spike went in, blood sprayed out of the guy's mouth and nose, away from Daniel. He didn't get one drop on himself. That was a first. He checked the pockets of the now dead suck-up and found two photos of himself in the company bathroom, holding a mirror covered in cocaine. He stuffed them into his pocket and stared down at the body. What should he do with the corpse? A wicked idea formed in his mind.

Several minutes later he stepped back and admired his work. He laid the body face down, pulled the pants to the ankles, and scattered the contents of the guy's wallet. He wanted it to look like the blackmailer had come here, possibly for some illicit gay sex, but got the business end of a spike instead. Daniel had already pocketed what money was in the wallet, but left the Rolex. He didn't want to get caught with that and have to explain himself.

Whistling, he walked back to his car and headed home. That was a couple of nights ago. The snitch's family had reported him missing, but the police hadn't yet found his body. Daniel only hoped he was in the office when the gossip started to churn around the "circumstances" of the man's death.

There was a soft knock on his office door.

"Yeah, c'mon in," Daniel called out.

Hap Simms, from Marketing, poked his head through the door. The man was seventy-five and should have retired years ago, but the company lacked the backbone to fire him or offer a severance package. Hap had no intention of quitting, so he still puttered around the office with barely enough work to keep him busy. Therefore he filled his time by going from office to office, checking in with everyone, and fueling the gossip windmill when necessary.

"You got a minute? You're not going to believe what I just heard."

Daniel's head snapped up, excited about the prospect of receiving news about his victim.

"Sure, Hap. What's going on?"

"Well, you know how Charles Daley went missing?"

David frowned. "Who?"

"You know that little kiss-ass from Finance."

"Oh, yeah. I thought his name was Jerry or something."

"No, it's Charlie. Anyway, seems the police found his body this morning."

"His body? You mean he's dead?"

"Yeah!" Hap exclaimed as he clapped his hands. "Apparently it was pretty gruesome. And that's not all."

He paused for dramatic effect. Daniel raised his eyebrows.

"And?"

"It seems our little brown-nosing, high and mighty, happily married man, was bare-assed naked from the waist down."

Daniel's eyes widened in feigned surprise. "No shit."

"Probably using petty cash to pay for a lady of the evening, if you know what I mean."

Hap stared at his shoes. He looked like he had more to say, but was embarrassed or unsure how to continue.

"Is there something else?"

"Well, the rumor is, considering the way his body was, uh, propped up, it may have been for one of those gay things."

"What do you mean, 'gay things'?" Daniel asked.

He knew how flustered Hap could get over the possibility of discussing the intricate details of a homosexual encounter.

"You know, maybe he wasn't paying for a lady of the evening, but a gentleman. He was hit in the back of the head, like maybe he was expecting someone to be behind him, you know?"

Daniel hid a smile. "You don't say."

"Well, *I* don't say. That's what everyone else is saying. Regardless, I suppose some of us should make an appearance at his funeral or wake or something."

"You're probably right, Hap. Do you know the details?"

"Not yet. I'm sure there will be a memo once the information is available."

"Right. Okay, thanks for the heads up. I'll see you later," Daniel waved as Hap scuttled down the hall to spread the news.

Later that afternoon, just as Hap predicted, HR circulated a memo, detailing the funeral information for what's-his-name, throughout the company. No wake, but the funeral would take place over the weekend. As a department head, Daniel thought he should attend. As the murderer, it would also be exciting to sit amongst the mourners, shedding his crocodile tears for the public.

On Saturday morning, he strolled into St. Thomas' church. Daniel spotted several people from work on the left-hand side of the main aisle and sat down behind them. As his coworkers whispered about the tragedy of it all and the awful nature of the man's death, Daniel looked around. He yawned at the detailed wooden carvings on the pews; he rolled his eyes at the beauty of the stained-glass windows. Just as he thought he would die of boredom in this house of God, he spotted a young woman across the aisle.

She was pixie-petite, pretty, with wavy chestnut hair, and large round eyes. Her delicate fingers were fiddling with the hymnal, and her eyes were searching the church. The person who sat on her right was speaking to her, but she appeared to be bored out of her skull and was looking for something to amuse her.

Daniel found that fascinating. To see someone like him, obviously not overly religious, or even spiritual, obligated to be here out of friendship or familial duty. She blew a lock of hair from her eyes in frustration just as her gaze fell on him. He smirked in amusement, to let her know that he felt the same way. One side of her mouth curled up in a smile, and a large dimple pierced her cheek. He heaved a deep sigh. He couldn't resist dimples.

The service began and everyone stopped talking to look at the priest. As with any religious service, Daniel tuned him out, and kept his full attention on the woman across the way. She, too, kept staring over at him. They held a secret conversation throughout the funeral with smiles, hand movements, and eye rolling.

The priest made an announcement at the end of the service to let everyone know that a brunch would be served at a local banquet hall for all the attendees. Daniel looked up at the ceiling and mouthed "amen" in thanks. He hadn't eaten this morning. Pixie-woman laughed as she saw this, but covered it up with a cough so no one would think her disrespectful. As the priest concluded the service, everyone stood to sing the final hymn. Then, finally, it was over, and all the congregants shuffled out of the church, their conversations muted out of respect for the dead or God or whatever.

Outside, Daniel lit up a cigarette, and stood off to the side. He watched the people file out of the church and mill around as they decided between returning to their offices or homes, or heading over to brunch. He spotted the pretty young woman who had sat across from him, and his heartbeat quickened. She walked over to him.

"I don't suppose you've got one of those to spare, do you?"

He nodded, and held out the open pack to her. She pulled out two. One she stuck behind her ear and the other she put in her mouth. Raising an eyebrow, he flipped open a Zippo lighter and lit the one in her mouth. She pulled deep on the cigarette and blew a cloud of blue smoke away from them. Seeing his expression as he twitched his chin toward the cigarette stuck behind her ear, she shrugged.

"Ah. You know, cigarettes are kinda like potato chips. You can't have just one. So instead of bothering you twice to bum one, I just figured I'd get it over with, and take two right from the get-go."

"I see. Makes sense."

"Besides, after that," she jerked her head back toward the church, "I'm going to need as many of these as I can get my hands on."

Daniel laughed, nodded, and lit another cigarette for himself. He leaned against a low stone post and stared at her. He always liked to play it smooth and aloof when it came to women. Let them instigate, do all the talking. That way he came off as more mysterious, fascinating, and that usually made women do anything to get to know him better. Like maybe go somewhere dark and secluded where he could do as he pleased, and have a convenient, out of the way place to dump the body later.

But to his surprise, she kept silent and continued to smoke her cigarette. Either she was shy, or was playing the same game as he. This intrigued him into doing something he normally didn't do – make the first move. He held out his hand to her.

"I'm Daniel, by the way, your cigarette supplier for this trip."

She laughed, a small soft sound, as she took his hand in hers. Her skin was smooth and silky. He wondered if the rest of her felt the same way.

"I'm Sylvia."

He blinked at the old-fashioned name that did not suit her at all. She laughed again.

"I know. ' Sylvia', right? I don't know what my mother was thinking."

"Well, are you an old-fashioned girl, Sylvia?"

She must have caught a slithery undertone to his question because she blinked and paused before responding. He knew his smile and clean-shaven, handsome face spoke volumes as to his trustworthy nature, but sometimes his eyes and his voice screamed sleaze ball. Whatever inner debate she had with herself seemed resolved as she gave him a lop-sided smile, flashing her dimple again.

"Hardly."

He raised his eyebrows and dropped his half-smoked cigarette onto the sidewalk, crushing it under his high-shine leather shoes. He held out his hand and gave her a half-bow.

"Then, my lady, may I suggest we get the hell out of here, and go grab some coffee?"

She curtseyed for him as she took his offered hand. "I know the perfect place."

They shared several cups of coffee and hours of conversation that afternoon. Daniel learned that she had been an RN at Mainland Hospital for the past five years. She liked heavy metal, Goth nightclubs, tattoos, Knob Creek whiskey, the recent fad of torture porn movies like 'Hostel', and the Teletubbies.

"I swear to God. I have no idea why I am so fascinated by those little buggers. If I'm flipping channels and I happen across one of their shows in progress, I'm stuck until it's over. It's almost like I can't change it once it's on, you know?"

Daniel had laughed for almost ten minutes over that. He'd never been so absorbed by a woman's company before. Everything about her was interesting or funny or just plain adorable. And even though he was enjoying himself, he knew this would only end up one way - with her death. But until that urge could no longer be suppressed, he was going to enjoy her company.

They met several times after that for more coffee or dinner. He never approached the topic of sex or even tried to move beyond second base with Sylvia. Daniel knew that once he did, he wouldn't be able to stop at just looking and feeling her body. He'd want to know how her entrails would glisten in the moonlight, or what patterns her blood would take as it slid down his skin. He'd need to know how loud she could scream in pain, for help, or for mercy.

He could tell Sylvia was getting a little frustrated. She kept pushing him for more. He continued to play the gentleman and refuse. Tonight, however, in the backseat of his car, she hammered the final nail in her own coffin.

"Daniel, what's going on?"

"What do you mean?"

"I mean, this. Us. Do you like me or don't you?"

"Honestly, Sylvia, I really do. I've never felt like this with any woman before."

"So then why are we not moving forward? And when I say 'moving forward', I mean 'having sex.'"

He blushed. He felt his face grow hot with the heat of his own rushing blood. He'd never done that before. It was too dark in the car to notice, though, so it was lost on her. Pity. It would have been nice to share that at least once with someone.

"It's because I like you that I'm not having sex with you."

Her face fell slack. "I'm not following."

"You don't understand, Sylvia. I become a different person when I start sleeping with someone. And I don't mean that I don't call anymore or I forget to show up for dates."

"Are you worried that you're going to hurt me, Daniel?"

"Yes."

She sniffed several times, then she wrapped her arms around his neck. He was confused by her reaction, but held her close, taking in her smell one more time before it became tainted with fear and pain.

"Daniel, that's got to be the nicest thing anyone's ever said to me. Most guys don't give a damn if they end up hurting the woman they're dating. They just want to get to the bump and grind and then figure out the fastest way to catch the next bus out of town."

She pulled away from him and caressed his face. "I'm a big girl, Daniel. I can take care of myself. Shit, I'm practically on the verge of raping you, so if I get hurt, it's only going to be my fault, right?"

Daniel mulled that sentiment over and nodded. "I guess so. Interesting mind you've got there, Sylvia."

She laughed. "It's not my mind I want you to be interested in."

He pinched her cheek and starting tucking in his shirt. She frowned.

"What are you doing?"

"Well, I'm not going to have our first time together be in the back seat of my Lincoln. I don't care how roomy it is."

She practically squealed with delight. She buttoned up her blouse and hopped out of the car. They both settled into the front seats and after she strapped on her seatbelt, she laid her hand on top of his.

"So, where are we going?"

Daniel smiled.

"Home."

He drove the car out of the secluded park toward home. Well, it wasn't his home, but she didn't need to know that. He knew of a secluded section of town where there were only a handful of houses and most of them were unoccupied. The housing slump hit all parts of the country hard, which served his particular needs. He'd been partial to a small ranch home at the end of a rough winding road and steered the car down that road now. Sylvia pointed up to a large house on their left.

"Eeeesh. That's a spooky house, isn't it? Who would live there?"

Daniel slowed the car down to look at the home. He'd passed it many times, but it still managed to creep him out every time he looked at it. A large Georgian style home that had probably once been a magnificent example of seventeenth-century architecture. It almost breathed a sense of foreboding and Daniel had a feeling that, even in its prime, it did the same. He imagined a high official or someone of great stature lived there in order to keep people in fear of him, keep them in line.

"No one. It's empty. Been empty for years, I guess. Luckily, that's not where we're going. We're headed down the road a bit."

"Good."

She shivered in her seat and he sped up to pass the monstrosity of a home that much faster. In another half a mile, he turned the car left into the narrow driveway of a red brick ranch. It had been built back in the seventies, but only two families ever occupied it. The last family that lived there moved out in 1980. No houses stood on either side, so it was easy to stash the 'For Sale' sign in the back while he was busy inside. No one would come snooping, not all the way out here, and not at night.

"This is your house? It's not exactly what I expected."

"What do you mean? It doesn't look like a bachelor pad?"

She pushed open her door, and slipped out of the car. "Not really. I expected you to be in a condo or something, I guess. Something more modern."

"Does that mean you don't want to go in?" he feigned disappointment as he leaned against the car.

She skipped around the front of the car and grabbed his hand. She pulled him behind her up to the front of the house.

"What do you think?"

Smiling, he pulled the copy of the stolen house key from his pocket and opened the front door. He stood to the side to let her enter first. He crossed the threshold and closed the door. As he turned one lock and pushed the deadbolt into place, he heard her sharp intake of breath.

"What?"

He turned back to face her and leaned against the door. He flipped the key up into the air and caught it, again and again, as his lips curled into a cruel smile.

"I'm sorry. My cleaning lady is off this week."

She whipped around to look at him, confusion and annoyance coloring her cheeks, but he could detect a hint of panic creeping around her eyes. She pointed at the sheet-covered furniture, what little there was, and swept her arm around to indicate the emptiness of a house that looked like it hadn't been lived in for years.

"What's going on here, Daniel? Is this some kind of joke?"

"No, not really. Well, not a joke on me, anyway."

The confusion faded and fear replaced the annoyance. She finally realized that this was not going to be a hot sensual night of sex and love. This empty home was to be her tomb. Her eyes darted from side to side. Her fight or flight instinct must have kicked in.

Daniel chuckled. "There's nothing here to help you, Sylvia. Believe me, I've taken every precaution. Just like I always do."

He let the truth of his words sink in. He always loved to see that deer in the headlights look when he told them what was going to happen. The disbelief, the denial, then the resignation of their impending deaths. Most of the time they accepted it without a fight. Some screamed and cried, or begged for their lives. Some even thought they could reason with him, as if they could convince him that he didn't need to do this. How could they reason with him when even he didn't know why he needed to kill?

But he could tell Sylvia was going to be a fighter. He had hoped for nothing less. Despite his desperate need to kill, he did feel a bit sad about having to lose Sylvia. If he had been a normal man, he supposed he could have fallen in love, married her, and they'd have lived happily ever after. Unfortunately for them both, he was not normal, and in order for this evening to end well, she had to die.

Watching her muscles tense for the coming fight, he circled to her left. She moved to her right. Her hands clenched into tight fists and she held them close to her chest. Her feet kept moving so she could be ready to dodge or turn when needed. Either she got in a lot of fights as a kid or she'd been taking boxing lessons for self-defense. They would just have to see how those will help her tonight.

He jumped toward her and she jumped back. He swiped his left fist then his right, but she dodged those as well. He smiled.

"Looks like someone here knows how to defend herself in a fight. Good for you, Sylvia. Good for you. I was hoping you'd give me a little more than the rest of them. Thank you."

"Fuck you, you son of a bitch!"

She swung her purse around slamming it against the side of his face. It wasn't a heavy handbag, but the zipper caught him in the eye and he cried in pain. He stumbled as he slapped a hand over his injury. She raised her heel and kicked it against his knee. He howled even louder. He fell, then rolled over onto his side, hugging his knee with one arm and covering his wounded eye with the other. She gave him a quick kick in the seat of his pants and ran for the door.

None of the locks on the inside required a key. She slammed back the deadbolt, twisted the second latch, and threw open the door to freedom. She risked a look back over her shoulder as Daniel rolled forward and tried to stand. He stumbled, but she didn't wait any longer. Sylvia turned forward and, pumping her arms and legs, headed for the road.

Grumbling and swearing, Daniel got to his feet. His eye watered, but it seemed undamaged. His knee, on the other hand, was another story. When he put weight on it, a streak of white-hot pain arced up to his hip and down to his ankle, but he couldn't afford to baby himself right now. His prey had escaped and if he didn't haul ass, he'd be in deep shit. He limped out the door after her.

She hadn't gotten far. He could make out her form as it weaved down the dirt road. A small plume of dust rose with every step as her feet pounded underneath her. He couldn't let her get too far ahead. If she got anywhere near town, someone might hear her if she started screaming. He yelled after her.

"Sylvia! I can see you, Sylvia. Why are you running? I just want to talk to you, sweetie!"

When she turned back to see how close on her heels he was, she tripped and fell. He smiled at his luck. He was able to close the distance between them while she struggled to get up. After she got back to her feet, she limped forward. She must have hurt her leg pretty badly. Good. Served the bitch right.

She screamed when she saw him close in. Just ahead was the monstrosity of a home they passed earlier, the one that had given her the creeps. She didn't care about that now because she made a beeline for it. She tripped again as she crossed the dead grass. Daniel caught up to her and flailed at her skirt as it whipped in the wind, but she jumped onto the porch steps before he could grab hold.

Sylvia looked back at him one more time as she threw herself against the front door. He couldn't imagine why she thought salvation laid within the old, abandoned home, but he wasn't interested in her thought process right now. All that mattered was that she didn't make it into town. She managed to push her way into the house and slam the door in his face. He heard a lock tumble into place, but he never broke his stride.

He bounced back off the closed door once, but he immediately rushed it again. The aged wood cracked under his weight and the molding gave way. The door flew open and he rolled into the foyer. He saw Sylvia standing in the living room off to the right, staring at him. He stood and smiled, panting from the chase.

"Sylvia, I've got to hand it to you. You really had me - what?"

He realized that she wasn't staring at him at all, but at someone or something behind him. He looked over his shoulder. As he did, he saw the intact front door, as if he'd never burst through a moment ago. A tingle of fear tickled the back of his neck. He thought a shadow passed close by, and he whipped around to track it. A floorboard creaked to his left, the original spot where Sylvia stared. He turned, expecting nothing. Just his imagination working overtime in the anticipation of the kill.

But it was not nothing. A swarm of shadows swirled and flew around the frail and pale figure of a young girl. Daniel bumped into Sylvia, not even realizing that he'd been backing away from the ghostly figure. Sylvia clutched his arm in a vise grip, apparently unconcerned that he had planned to kill her a moment ago. He gripped her hands in his, not wanting to find comfort in her death now, but in her life, and he believed she wanted the same.

The only thing they found tonight was an eternity of hell.

ROSALIE
(MODERN DAY)

Rosalie poked at the dead frog with a small stick. It floated on its back in the small pond, a white string of guts trailing from its mouth. Severe rainstorms had flooded this field earlier in the spring, but all that remained this August afternoon was a pond that more resembled a deep puddle. She didn't know why the frog wasn't hopping around the field, making little frogs, and hanging out with all his frog friends. She wondered what had killed it.

Rosalie may have only been nine years old, but she understood death. She had seen it, up close in all its dark and shrouded glory. Six months ago, she had watched her mother die. They were driving home from the grocery store on a cold, clear February afternoon. The sky mirrored the soft hue of her mother's eyes. She and her mother planned a 'girl's day' together. Rosalie wanted to make banana splits, so her mother drove them to the store to pick up three kinds of ice cream, chocolate fudge sauce, peanuts, cherries, and of course, bananas. Her mother also bought fixings for homemade pizza, Rosalie's favorite food.

Under the pretense of safeguarding the ice cream, Rosalie convinced her mother to put the banana split fixings on the back seat next to her, instead of in the trunk. Secretly she wanted to pop open the squeeze bottle of fudge sauce, and sample the rich treat before they got home. Her mother probably knew what Rosalie planned, but she obliged her young daughter anyway.

Rosalie never got the chance to sample the chocolate, or anything else that day. As she sat in the back, behind the passenger's seat, she eyed her mother, waiting for the perfect moment to bend over and snatch the fudge sauce bottle from the bag at her feet. Her mother's hair bobbed and swayed as she maneuvered the car through the parking lot and onto the busy street, careful to avoid pedestrians and other cars. Her blue eyes sparkled in the review mirror each time she checked on Rosalie, possibly to check for hot fudge drippings painting her daughter's chin.

Rosalie thought her chance had arrived when the car slowed to a stop at a red light. Her mother watched her in the review mirror, smiling, and Rosalie thought she was the most beautiful woman in the whole world. Happy that she shared the same clear eyes and golden hair, she smiled back at her mom as the car moved through the intersection.

Rosalie couldn't remember the exact moment of impact. She heard a loud screech as metal scraped against metal. The grill of a hulking SUV tried to force its way into the driver's seat. An explosion of glass sprayed a prismed specter across her mother's face before it sliced the flesh into tattered ribbons. Blood flew from her mother's mouth, across the front seat.

The seatbelt over her mother's body had kept her secure, preventing her from being thrown from the behind the steering wheel and through the passenger window. It locked at the moment of impact. The taut fabric crushed her ribs with a series of cracks, and dislocated her left shoulder. Her head, neck, and right arm seemed to stretch beyond any human capacity, like they wanted to fly out the window, but the rest of her ravaged body wouldn't cooperate.

In the end, her right fist burst through the passenger window. Her neck twisted and snapped to the left. As the force of the collision finally slowed, her mother's body sagged out from behind the seatbelt. Her head, now facing the rear window, came to rest on the back of the passenger seat. A quiet sigh of breath whispered through her mother's bloodied lips.

"Rosalie."

Her name. The last word her mother spoke was her daughter's name. She forgot all about the hot fudge sauce as she unlocked her own seatbelt, and sat forward. Her mother's beautiful blue eyes lost their shine. The right one had filled with blood. She touched her mother's cheek as tears streamed down her face, and into her mouth. Her mother forced a weak smile, then Death brushed His hand across her face, forever freezing it in that gentle countenance.

Rosalie never forgot that moment, the soft beauty of her mother's smile while salt burned her own tongue with bitterness would forever be etched in her memory. It seemed like hours passed as she sat there caressing her mother's cheek, staring into her beautiful dead face, before she was pulled out of the car and put into an ambulance. It was only then that Death's spell had finally broken, and the pain pushed forward.

She never felt the impact, but her head had whipped to the right and cracked the window. Blood crept down her temple, over her cheek and jaw, and she never even noticed. On the way to the hospital, the emergency technician cleaned and inspected the wound. A rivulet of blood trickled over her lips. Her tongue slipped along her bottom lip as she took a quick taste. She had once put a penny in her mouth to see if it tasted as shiny as it looked. Her blood had the same metallic flavor. Perhaps a bit smoother, a bit sweeter. Rosalie licked her lips completely clean so she could savor all the tiny nuances in her blood. She wondered if her mother's had tasted the same.

Rosalie never found out. She didn't see her mother again until the wake. Why it was called a 'wake', she didn't know. Her mother wasn't asleep, or planning to wake up when everyone got there. Even as Rosalie poked and prodded the body, her mother didn't twitch. Her father became frantic, and dragged her outside to scold her.

He must have though she didn't understand the difference between sleep and death because he spoke to her in a slow, deliberate manner. He went on and on about final rest, heaven, God, and something about angels. After several minutes of his lecture, she stopped listening, and nodded her head over and over. That seemed to make him happy, and he finally stopped talking and took her back inside.

She remembered that day as she poked at the frog. Everyone seemed so uncomfortable. No one looked at her mother's body as it lay in the coffin, unless they were kneeling in front of it and praying. Even then she noticed everyone looked at the flowers, the picture of her mother from her wedding day, the coffin, the walls, anything but the body itself. She found that so peculiar. Were they afraid? Were they disgusted? She wanted to know.

After her father brought her back inside, she sat next to her grandma. Maybe Rosalie could talk to her about death, even though half of the time she seemed to be somewhere else. In her head anyway.

"Granny?"

The old woman stared ahead at the blank wall next to the casket. She wasn't so much avoiding the body. She seemed to deny the very reality of her daughter's death.

"Granny?" Rosalie repeated.

The old woman blinked, rousing herself from the numbness of grief.

"Hmmm? Yes, Rosalie. What is it, dear?"

"Why did mom die?"

Her grandmother frowned, and swallowed. "It's hard to know God's plan, Rosalie. Sometimes, sometimes He calls us home without telling us why."

"No, I mean," Rosalie started to ask again.

"But don't you worry, sweetheart. Your mommy is in Heaven now, and will always watch over you."

"But-"

Her grandmother dissolved into a series of sobs and wails. Her Aunt Muriel rushed over, pulling Rosalie away, and frowning at her.

"What did you do, Rosalie? What did you say to her?"

"I didn't do anything. I just asked her why my mom died."

"You what? What is wrong with you? Her daughter just died. Can't you be a little more thoughtful?" Muriel clutched at her dress collar as she stared down at Rosalie.

Rosalie pursed her lips and frowned, trying to display what she hoped was the fiercest scowl she could muster. "Well it was *my mom* that just died, Aunt Muriel. Why can't *you* be more thoughtful?"

Before her aunt could respond, Rosalie turned on her heel, and strode out of the wake. She walked out to the lobby, and sat down on one of the overstuffed sofas near the front window. She wiped at her eyes before the tears could spill down her cheeks. Uncle Brian, her father's brother, sat down next to her, and put his arm around her shoulders.

"Don't you mind your Aunt Muriel, Rosalie. She's just upset."

"She only worries about grandma and herself. Mom wasn't her daughter or even her real sister. Technically, she's not even related. If she hadn't married Uncle Carl, she wouldn't even be here."

Her uncle covered a small smile with his hand then cleared his throat.

"Well, just between you and me, I never liked her either. Ever since Carl brought her home to meet the family, she's been a big pain in the butt."

Rosalie smiled up at her uncle. She could always count on him to make her feel better.

"Uncle Brian, why did my mom die?"

He squeezed her close. "I don't know, Rosalie. Some people believe that God determines how long we're allowed to live. Some think it's all random and accidental that we even exist. I personally believe that there is some kind of plan in place for us, but a monkey wrench gets thrown in from time to time."

"So was her death part of the plan, or one of those monkey wrenches?"

"I wish I knew, Rosalie."

"Uncle Brian, have you ever seen anyone die before?"

He glanced down at her. "Actually, I have."

"Tell me about it."

"Well, when I was on the police force, I was called into a robbery situation at a local convenience store. Some punk got in over his head, and ended up holding the clerk at gunpoint. One thing led to another, and by the time it was all over, I'd shot the guy."

"The robber?"

"Yep. I'll spare you all the gory details."

"No, don't."

"Don't what?" he asked as he looked down at her.

"Don't spare me. Tell me everything. I want to know."

"Why do you want to know?"

Rosalie chewed on her bottom lip. Ever since her mother died, she had become intensely curious about death in all its forms. She'd taken to sitting in her basement for hours as spiders built their webs, their death traps, for any unlucky insect that happened to fall into them. It was fascinating to watch the process the spiders took in sucking the life from their prey, or wrapping them up for later. She also studied the bug corpses stuck in her windowsill. Not the spider victims, but the ones that got trapped in the house and couldn't find their way out.

Talking to her uncle, as someone who had witnessed death, or even caused it, would help her to understand it. But could she trust him enough to listen, or would he be scared? She decided in the end that she would trust him, and hope for the best.

"Tell me about the robber."

He paused while he closed his eyes and remembered that afternoon.

"The robber couldn't have been more than eighteen, but like most teenagers, he thought he knew everything about the world. Walking into a corner store with a gun meant that everything would go his way and he'd get what he wanted. Unfortunately, what one wants and what one gets can sometimes be two different things.

"When I arrived on the scene, the kid already had his arm around the clerk's neck, and the gun pointed at the terrified man's temple. He was screaming at the two other customers, even though they were already cowering on the floor. I tried to calm him down, but because things had gone so wrong for him, he probably thought he couldn't get out of there alive."

"Guess he was right, huh?"

Her uncle stared down at her, and tucked a stray lock of hair behind her ear. "I guess so. When he pointed his gun at me, I had no choice but to shoot him. He still had the clerk in his arm, so I aimed for the kid's leg. Luckily, I'm a good shot and when the bullet hit, he let go of his hostage and fell to the floor. I thought that would be it and he'd give up. But no such luck, for either of us.

"He raised his gun up and aimed it at one of the other customers on the floor. A little girl, younger than you are now. So I had no choice this time. I had to put him down for good."

"Where'd you shoot him?"

"In the head."

"Was there a lot of blood?"

"Mmm hmm. It was the first time I ever used my gun, so I had no idea what to expect. I'd never seen so much blood before. It," he paused and stared at her. "I'm not so sure I should be talking to you about this."

"No, please, Uncle Brian. Tell me."

He looked around to make sure no one was listening in on their conversation. Then he turned to her with a light in his eyes.

"It was disturbing to see so much blood, but at the same time, I was fascinated by it all. The smell of it, the color. It was so bright against the white tile of the floor, kinda like a candy apple, you know?"

Rosalie nodded. "I do."

Her uncle stroked her cheek in sympathy. He knew that Rosalie had been trapped in the accident wreckage with her mother's corpse for hours before being rescued.

"Is that why you want me to tell you all this? Because of the accident and your mom's death?"

She nodded again, looking up at him. She could feel her eyes widen as she spoke.

"It's all I think about. I even dream about it. I see mom's body. I can taste my blood on my lips, and it makes me feel happy. I want more."

Her uncle's mouth dropped into an 'O' of surprise. He swallowed hard, and looked around again to make sure no one was listening. He pulled Rosalie closer.

"Now listen to me, Rosalie. Don't ever tell anyone what you just told me. About the blood, I mean. No one will understand, you hear? You keep that to yourself, or they'll think you're nuts and lock you up."

Rosalie let out a sigh of defeat. She thought Uncle Brian would understand, but he only looked scared. He cupped her chin and gave her a secret smile.

"I know what you're thinking. And no, I'm not afraid of you. I'm afraid for you. It'll be tough to keep your desires a secret. Believe me, I know."

Rosalie felt the weight of a million bricks lift from her shoulders, and she threw her arms around her uncle's neck. He squeezed her tightly, and whispered to her.

"It'll be all right, Rosalie. I can help you. We can help each other."

Since that day, Rosalie's Uncle helped her to discover the vast reaches of her fascination with blood, and ultimately, death. They combed neighborhoods, woods, parks, any place where they might find it. Today, Rosalie was on her own. As she poked the frog, she thought of her Uncle and when she might get a chance to tell him about it.

On the far side of the field, an older boy, probably in high school, ran out from a dense copse of trees, followed by three more boys the same age. Even from her distant spot, Rosalie could see the terror in the first boy's expression as he ran for his life. Unfortunately, one of the boys giving chase caught up within a half dozen yards, and tackled him. Once he was down, the remaining two boys stopped running, and doubled over to catch their breath.

As they sauntered over to the captured boy, one of them looked around the field, as if making sure no one else was around. Rosalie flattened out onto her stomach, hoping the tall grass and weeds surrounding her would be enough to conceal her presence. The boy seemed satisfied, and turned his attention back to his prey.

He said something to his friends, and they laughed, but Rosalie couldn't hear from her hiding place. The boy on the ground tried to get up, but all three of his pursuers kicked him down. He yelled in pain. His yells quickly turned to screams. Then he was silent. The three boys didn't stop their assault for several minutes, and one of them bent down to punch his victim in the face, over and over again.

When they had each finished their vicious attack, they stood over the motionless boy. Rosalie couldn't tell if they were gloating in success, or stunned by their own ferocity. One of the boys pushed his foot against the body, as if daring the boy to get up and take another beating. When their target didn't respond, the three boys exchanged looks. One of them bent down, and put his head against the beaten boy's chest. He jumped up in a panic and this time, Rosalie could hear him.

"Holy shit, he's dead!"

The three boys argued for a few minutes, after each one had checked the body for any sign of life. They looked around the field, and Rosalie pressed herself against the ground again. When she heard the pounding run of their retreat, she raised her head. She saw them just as they disappeared into the thicket of maples, oaks, and low scrubby bushes.

She got to her knees, and watched the wooded area where the boys disappeared. Satisfied that they weren't coming back, she approached the dead body, the frog forgotten with this new and exciting opportunity. Stick still in hand, she stood over the boy and poked his arm. Yep, he was dead all right.

Spatters and streaks of blood covered his clothes. What she supposed was his face looked more like a red balloon filled with lumpy oatmeal, and a small pool of blood filled a crater in the center. She dipped a slender finger into the viscous liquid, and held it under her nose. A sharp tang filled her nostrils. Would it taste the same as hers?

Rosalie raised her hand, and held the wet finger over her head. A large drop of blood hung suspended for a moment, the sun bouncing off its surface with a pink gleam. It broke free, and fell into her mouth. She closed her lips, and worked her tongue back and forth, coating it in the boy's blood. It tasted similar to hers, but this was much sharper, with a bit of a sour undertone. To be sure, she stuck her whole finger in her mouth, and licked it clean.

The sour tang overwhelmed her taste buds and she spat out as much as she could. Why did his blood taste so different from her own? Was it the difference in age, sex, all that running he did? She'd have to talk it over with Uncle Brian. Maybe he'd know.

She skipped back home, the warm afternoon breeze blowing through her flouncing hair, and found it empty. Her father had gone to the store and not yet returned. Good. She'd have the chance to talk to Uncle Brian before he'd have to call the police.

I'm just a scared little girl who lost her mother only six months ago. No one was home so I could only think to call my uncle, the former policeman. He'd know what to do. She smirked as she dialed his number.

A month after tasting the dead boy, school started up again. Rosalie's father wanted her to go back to a normal life as soon as possible, but he never pressured her, in anything. If she didn't want to talk, fine; if she wanted to go off alone, that was okay, too; if she didn't want to go back to school, he was satisfied. As long as she was happy, so was he.

But Rosalie wanted to go. It was boring hanging around the house all day, or even exploring the nearby woods and park. There were only so many times she could come home late, to "accidentally" break the good china, and still not get a rise out of her father. It was fun at first, watching him struggle with the dilemma of whether or not punishing or reprimanding her would do more harm than good, especially after all she'd been through. Even after she started pulling the wings off dragonflies, and setting intricate and painful traps for the local wildlife, he turned a blind eye. He literally let her get away with murder.

So Rosalie needed more challenging stimuli, and thought school would be the best place to find it. Just her luck, on the first day, she found what she was looking for. Alisa. Alisa was small for her age, and painfully shy. While all the other kids ran around to talk to friends, or make new ones, Alisa stood off to the side, picking at a button on her sweater, disregarded by everyone.

Rosalie ignored her old friends, and walked over to Alisa.

"Hi."

Alisa's head snapped up at the sound of Rosalie's voice. She looked confused as she scanned for kids standing behind her.

"Are you t..t...talking to m...me?"

Rosalie had no idea that Alisa stuttered. An unexpected amusement, it only made the girl appear weaker. Rosalie smiled, satisfied that she had found the perfect subject for the experiment brewing in her brain. Alisa mistook that predatory smile for one of friendship, and smiled back.

"You're Alisa, right?"

"Uh-huh. And you're R...R...Rosalie."

"Yep, that's me. So whose homeroom are you in this year?"

"M...M...Mrs. Blackstone. What ab..b..bout you?"

"Same here. Cool. Wanna sit next to each other?"

Alisa's mouth dropped in surprise. Rosalie could imagine that no one had ever wanted to sit with Alisa before. She nodded so hard that her long, stringy curls bounced and bobbed, a few catching in the corner of her gaping mouth. The morning bell rang, and Rosalie grabbed Alisa's hand.

"C'mon, let's go."

As they walked hand in hand down the hallway, their classmates stared at the pair in confusion, muttering and whispering to each other.

After several long weeks of convincing Alisa that she really wanted to be her friend, Rosalie decided to put her experiment into action. One Saturday afternoon, while she and Alisa were watching television at her house, Rosalie nudged the girl with her elbow.

"I'm bored. Wanna go exploring?"

"Exploring? W...w...where?"

Forever Trapped

"How about - sshhh. Wait, here comes my dad."

Rosalie's father trotted down the stairs and into the kitchen next to the family room where the girls watched TV. He called out to them.

"Girls? You having fun in there?"

"Yeah, dad."

He pulled a ring of keys off the wall by the phone, and walked into the family room. He collected his wallet and money clip from the fireplace mantle.

"I've got to run into work for about an hour. Will you two be okay alone?"

"Sure."

"Good. Maybe I'll bring pizza home on my way back."

"Okay."

He seemed almost relieved by the annoyance in her voice, something any 'normal' child would do when trying to hang out with friends, only to have a parent constantly interrupting. He blew Rosalie a quick kiss, and headed out the door. Alisa smiled.

"He seems really n...n...nice."

Rosalie rolled her eyes. "Whatever. Do you want to go exploring or not?"

"W...w...where?"

"The old house on the cliff, outside of town."

Alisa paled. "The h...h...haunted h...h...house?"

Rosalie smirked. "You don't really believe in ghosts, do you, Alisa?"

"Well…"

"'Cause that's kinda babyish, don't you think? No wonder you don't have any friends."

Rosalie's remarks elicited the exact reaction she'd hoped for. Alisa's eyes spilled over with tears, then she sniffed and wiped at her face. Rosalie relaxed her expression, hoping to emulate a guilty countenance.

"I'm sorry, Alisa. I didn't really mean that. Besides, I'm your friend, right? So how could I say that you don't have any?"

Alisa smiled and nodded. As she took the tissue Rosalie offered and dabbed at her eyes, Rosalie's smile returned.

"C'mon, Alisa. Please? Please go with me to the house. I won't let anything happen to you, I swear."

Alisa laughed, but Rosalie was counting on Alisa willing to face a million ghosts rather than lose her only friend.

"All r…r…right."

"Sweet. Let's go!"

By the time they approached the house, Rosalie wanted to choke the life out of Alisa. It was like a verbal floodgate had been opened, and Alisa talked non-stop during the entire walk. If Rosalie hadn't already planned to torture and kill her in the seclusion of the abandoned house, she might have grabbed the nearest rock and bashed Alisa's skull in a hundred times over by now. Maybe she was covering her fear with all this talk. Maybe she was over excited that someone wanted to hang out with her. Rosalie just wanted it to stop.

The sight of the dark abandoned home managed to hit the mute button on Alisa's chatter. She slowed her footsteps until she came to a stop at the front steps. Rosalie had already climbed up to the porch and looked down at Alisa, disgust flaming her annoyance into anger.

"C'mon already. You're not still scared, are you?"

Alisa shook her head, and took one step up toward the porch. Rosalie snorted in derision, then reached down to grab Alisa's hand. She yanked the smaller girl up to the porch with such force that Alisa cried out in pain, her fear temporarily forgotten.

"Ow!"

"Geez, you're such a baby. Let's go inside."

Rosalie pulled open the rusty screen only to find the front door locked. Blowing a strand of stray hair from her eyes, she stood with her hands on her hips while she tried to figure a way inside. Alisa looked relieved, but it was short-lived. Rosalie spotted a brick near one of the front windows. She crowed in triumph, and dragged Alisa over to it.

"Perfect! We'll go in through the window."

"B...b...but Rosalie..."

"But nothing. Nobody lives here, so who cares if we break one little window? Look, no one's around to see us, either. Let's do it."

Rosalie threw the brick through the darkened window. It shattered, and jagged shards of glass rained down with singsong *plinks* to the porch. She laid her jacket over the edge of the sill, and turned to Alisa.

"Okay, I'll help you up, then you can pull me in."

Alisa opened her mouth to object, but Rosalie shoved her toward the opening. She bent her legs and lifted the smaller girl. Alisa placed one foot on the sill and the other through the window, bracing it on something just below Rosalie's line of sight. She turned back, and held out her hand. Rosalie reached for the it, and both girls tumbled inside.

Seconds later, a young woman jogged up the hill with her dog. She stopped in front of the empty house to take her pulse. As she studied her watch, her dog stared at the home, a low growl rumbling in his throat. The young woman stopped counting her heart beats, and stared up at the house. Nothing looked out of place. Granted, it was a bit run down, the dead lawn a crusty eyesore. But the wooden planks seemed solid, the roof was intact, and the unbroken windows glinted in the afternoon sun. Frowning, she tugged on the dog's leash.

"What is it, Roscoe? You see a squirrel or something? C'mon, let's head back."

She tugged the leash again, and the dog followed her back down the hill. From inside the old, abandoned home, Alisa and Rosalie pounded on the window glass, screaming.

MURIEL SPENCER
(1975)

Muriel upturned the plastic gallon bucket and dumped the contents into the old well in her backyard. Blood splashed on the low rock wall as she struggled with the weight of the container. A skinny loop of intestine stuck to ledge. Once empty, she lowered the bucket to the ground, and slipped the slim flashlight from between her dentures. They had started to slip as she clenched the metal cylinder. She really needed to find a new adhesive.

She plucked the stranded entrails off the low rock wall and tossed them into the well. How she wished she could have heard the soft *plsssh* as it hit the low water at the bottom. But at seventy-eight years old, her hearing wasn't what it used to be. She just counted her blessings that she could even carry all this slop out here by herself. Heaven forbid she'd ever have to take on a partner. Then she'd have to share in all the fun of killing, not just the burdens of clean-up.

She carried the empty bucket over to the spigot at the back of the house. After placing it below the pipe, Muriel turned on the water. The bucket would need rinsing before she could take it back into the house. It wouldn't do to drip any blood onto the linoleum. Aside from being irresponsible, she just cleaned the floors yesterday. She took the bucket back over to the well and dumped the ruddy water into it. Muriel did this two more times before she felt it was clean enough to take inside.

It was hard work, albeit necessary. Her bones ached and her fingers cramped, but if it kept her secrets secret, it was all worth it. She eased the side door open and placed the bucket on the steps leading down to the basement. Two stairs on her right led up to her kitchen and she climbed them with some effort. She shuffled over to a mustard yellow, vinyl kitchen chair and eased her body into it to take a moment of rest.

For Muriel's age, no one could complain about her shape. She walked several miles every day and took care of a small garden at the side of her home. Even her extracurricular activities kept her healthy, but slopping blood and water back and forth to the well wore her out. Taking a few minutes of rest at her kitchen table was all she needed to feel better.

Once she caught her breath, she stood and headed for the basement. She picked up the bucket on her way downstairs. The old steps creaked under her weight. Once she reached the bottom, Muriel put the bucket in the far corner with the others, then turned toward the far side of the room which had been sectioned off by heavy, glass sliding doors. A large steel tub sat against the wall across from the doors.

She grabbed rubber gloves, lined with PVC, from a small clip on the wall. Once she slipped them on, she took the gas mask from a nearby hook and pulled it over her face. Harold had been so thoughtful to get two masks from the Army/Navy store all those years ago. Her late husband had always been so generous and thoughtful of others, even more so for his wife, with whom he wanted to share everything. Especially his love of homicide.

Muriel flipped a switch on the wall next to the masks to turn on the venting fan in the ceiling. It pulled the fumes from the hydrochloric acid up and out through the attic. Only when the fan engaged did she open the sliding door and approach the metal tub. She grabbed a length of PVC pipe leaning against the wall and stirred it around the pool of crimson liquid. She heard a muffled clank as the pipe bumped against a remnant of bone at the bottom of the tub. If she left it in the acid for one more night, it should be dissolved by morning.

She stripped off the gloves and mask after she stepped out of the enclosed room. She had already cleaned the rest of the basement earlier, so she felt good about heading off to bed. Just as she reached the steps, she heard a muffled thump behind her. She turned and stared at the young girl tied to the rocking chair in the corner. One of her feet had come loose from the thick rope that bound it to the arced rocker on the bottom. Her dark eyes glared at Muriel and she muffled curses behind the gag.

"Dammit. I could have sworn I gave you enough sedative to last through the night."

Muriel shook her head and walked to the cabinet on the wall next to the girl. She opened the middle drawer and pulled out a syringe already filled with her homemade cocktail of fentanyl and heroin. The girl kicked her foot forward, swinging it back and forth, but was unable to reach Muriel.

Muriel leaned in and injected the drugs into the girl's neck. Within seconds, she stopped kicking and her head fell forward as she slumped into unconsciousness. Muriel put the empty syringe back in the cabinet and bent down to re-tie the girl's leg to the chair.

She winced at the sound of her popping knee joints as she stood. She'd better take a few aspirin before bed so she wouldn't pay for all this activity tomorrow. Muriel still had a lot of work to do with this one.

After slowly climbing the stairs, Muriel made her way to her bedroom. She walked to her dresser and opened the top drawer. She pulled out a flat wooden box and sat down on the bed, as she'd done nearly every night since Harold died. The top of the box was decorated with a painted scene of Siesta Key Beach in Florida. Small waves rolled toward the dry sand as sea gulls soared through a blue sky. A dark pelican dotted the horizon and a flock of sand pipers scrabbled at the water line. She ran her hand across the top of the box as she remembered the vacation she and Harold had taken when they purchased this trinket.

She raised the lid and ruffled her fingers through the mementos she and Harold had gathered over the years. Muriel picked up a soft velvet pouch and pulled the strings apart, opening the bag. She turned it upside down and a handful of teeth spilled out into her palm. Molars, bicuspids, canines, some dotted with silver or encased in gold, some pure and untouched by decay. She held up a flat tooth, encrusted with two diamonds, to the light. It sparkled and flashed as she remembered the young woman who wore it. She had been high on meth when she tried to mug Muriel and Harold. But he had gotten the drop on her, despite the fifty-year age difference.

Smiling, she put the teeth back in the pouch and picked up a cylinder of soft cotton cloth, stained with brown splotches. She unrolled it and exposed the index finger of a white middle-aged man. The gold nugget ring still adorned the digit. Harold had gotten a bruise on his lip, that matched the ring's pattern after the man slugged him, which took weeks to heal. It had only been a defensive move. Harold attacked him first. Not because of any ill-doing on the man's part or some misunderstood offense. Harold just felt like killing him and adding him to the collection.

Muriel rolled up the cloth and tucked it back into the box. She touched a few other souvenirs – a mummified tongue, a few leathery remnants of eyeballs, a scrap of scalp, a small glass jar of fingernails – before closing the lid and putting it back in her drawer.

She slipped out of her housedress and into a white floor-length nightgown adorned with pale pink roses. She turned down the covers on one side of the bed then slipped between the cool sheets. Rolling over, Muriel pulled the sheets up around Harold's chin. The skin around his skull had pulled away from the bone due to shrinkage, and his copper and white hair was dull. She made a mental note to wax his mummified skin and add some oil to his lifeless hair as she placed a kiss on his leathery cheek.

"Good night, darling."

Cheryl sat in her car parked outside the small bungalow home. She sucked and blew cigarette smoke continually as she stared at the house. The lawn was neatly manicured and the small garden by the front steps was meticulous in its design and color scheme. Its appearance fooled the outside world that the old lady living here was as benign as banana bread. But Cheryl knew the truth. Cheryl knew the old woman was a killer granny.

Luce, fidgeting in the passenger seat and bored to tears, nudged Cheryl.

"Are we just going to sit here all night or what? I'm bored. Let's go do something."

"We are doing something. We're watching the enemy."

Luce frowned and stared at the little house. "The enemy? In there? Are you serious?"

Cheryl nodded as she blew out more blue grey smoke. "She's got Stell in there for sure. She might still have Bobby, but I think she hauled his guts out last night."

"What the hell are you talking about, Cher?"

Cheryl pointed her cigarette at the small house. "That old lady in there is a killer. She got Bobby and Stell a few nights ago when they tried to break in."

"Uh, how would you know that?"

"Because I was driving the damn car, bitch. How the hell else would I know? They went in, but they never came back out. I been watching the old bat ever since."

"Okaaay."

Cheryl blew smoke in Luce's face. "Look, you turkey. You don't have to believe me, but that doesn't make it any less true. I'm going to go take a peek in them windows and see what I can see. You wait here and keep the car running."

She slipped out from behind the wheel and eased the driver's door closed. As she walked around the front of the car, Luce rolled down the passenger window.

"But Cher-"

Cheryl whipped around and thrust her hand through the open window. She grabbed Luce by her long dark hair and pulled her head back hard enough to make the girl's neck snap in protest. She whispered her orders.

"Just stay here and keep the motor on. If you see me tear ass down the street, take off and meet me back at the apartment. You got that?"

Luce barely managed a nod in response and Cher pushed the girl's head away. Luce rubbed her neck and winced, but didn't say another word. Cher darted across the street and into the old woman's yard. As luck would have it, no nearby streetlights shone on her as she made her way to the side of the house and bent down to peer into the basement windows.

She moved from window to window, but she couldn't see much of anything. Streaks of dark and light marred each pane of glass, as if they had been painted on the inside. At the last window, however, Cheryl could see through a narrow sliver of clear glass that hadn't been obscured. It was dark, but she saw something in the far corner. Squinting, Cheryl leaned in, and held her hands up against the sides of her face.

She couldn't make out any specific details, but she thought the dark shape looked like a girl sitting in a chair. Her head hung forward, as if she were asleep or drugged. Cheryl pulled out the penlight from her back pocket and held a hand over it as she switched it on. She pointed it at the basement window and leaned in to see if it would illuminate the gloom of the basement.

Cheryl sucked in a deep breath as she recognized Stell. She couldn't see her face, but she recognized the straight, jet black hair and the clothes she'd been wearing a few nights ago. She didn't see Bobby anywhere and assumed she was right about the old lady hauling his guts out earlier that evening. A tear rolled down Cheryl's face as she thought about her friends trapped in this house.

She wiped it away and stood. The bitch wasn't going to get away with it. Cher would find a way to get even with her, even if she had to kill the old bat herself. She strode back to the car and yanked open the driver's door. She threw herself behind the wheel and slammed the door shut. Luce jumped and stared at her.

"So?"

"Stell's in there."

"What? Well, what are we gonna do? We can't just leave her!"

Cher glared at her friend.

"Don't worry, Luce. I've got a plan. I just hope the old bitch falls for it before anything more happens to Stell. C'mon. We've got work to do."

The two girls stood out in front of the old, weathered home on the edge of town. Despite its age, it was still in good shape. The roof remained intact and all the windows had miraculously escaped the handiwork of the local vandals. From the bottom of the front steps it was difficult, if not impossible, to see inside the home. Perfect. She nudged Luce in the ribs.

"This is the place."

Luce shivered. "Place for what?"

Cheryl glared at the younger girl who shrunk back.

"What the hell have we been talking about for the past two days, Luce? God, you're such an idiot sometimes. We're going to lure the old bag out here and take care of her. We're gonna get revenge on that bitch for Bobby, Stell, and anyone else she's killed."

Luce blew out a long breath into the cold afternoon air.

"So what do you want me to do?"

"You get in there and block up the windows. They're pretty dark, but it wouldn't hurt to paint 'em over or something. Also, take the supplies with you. It'll make the old bat suspicious if I show up with a bag full of stuff when I threaten blackmail."

Luce nodded. "When do you want me to start setting up?"

Cher walked back to the car and pulled a heavy duffle bag from the trunk. She zipped it open to check over its contents: rope, duct tape, pliers, an ice pick, plastic baggies with various narcotics, and a box of syringes. She zipped it closed and carried it to Luce.

Cher shoved the bag at her friend and the girl stumbled.

"Now. I'll go to the old lady and set up the meeting for tonight."

Luce gulped as she stared up at the large house in fear.

"You want me to stay alone in there all day by myself?"

Cher slapped the girl hard across the cheek. When Luce gaped at her, Cher hit her again then shoved her toward the steps. When the girl hesitated, Cher grabbed her by the back of her coat and hauled her up to the porch. She yanked open the screen and pushed on the front door. It opened.

As Cher stared at the open door in surprise, Luce tried to wriggle free. Lucky break, she thought, before shoving Luce inside.

"Now get to work."

Before Cher could reach for the door, it slammed in her face. She couldn't be sure, but it seemed the door closed on its own. Dismissing the idea, Cher assumed Luce had done it to piss her off. She thought she heard Luce screaming, but it stopped almost as soon as it began.

Shrugging, Cheryl strolled down to the car and drove back through town to the old woman's house. By this time tomorrow, the bitch would be dead, or at least begging for death. If Stell was still alive, Cher could help her once the old bag was out of the way.

Cher maneuvered her Pinto down the old woman's street and pulled into her driveway. She turned off the engine and took a deep breath, steeling her resolve. Anger flared in her chest when she pictured Stell slumped over and tied to a chair in the woman's basement. Cher threw open her door and strode up to the house.

She pulled the baseball cap she wore down over her eyes as she knocked. She could hear a faint response from within the house, something like, "Just a moment." Cher stuffed her hands in her coat pockets, trying to look casual and to wrap her hand around the switchblade she'd tucked inside.

After a minute, the front door creaked open and Cher was finally face to face with the old woman. For some reason Cher expected her to look different up close, but the woman who stood before her seemed as innocuous and sweet as her own grandmother. She wore a blue and grey flowered housedress and tan support shoes. Her snow-white hair was curled in a short, tight permanent. Her skin, though deeply lined, glowed with a healthy pink color. The woman's eyes, bright and deep blue, were the only things belying her innocent façade. They were the eyes of a predator.

"Yes? May I help you?"

Cher gripped the blade tighter for comfort and support.

"Mrs. Spencer?"

"Yes, who are you?"

"My name is Cheryl and I believe you're holding my friend captive in your basement."

Muriel blinked once. Cher's lips twitched. She had caught the old woman off guard, though she quickly recovered and smiled.

"I'm afraid I don't understand, dear."

It was Cheryl's turn to smile.

"Oh I think you do, Mrs. Spencer."

Muriel's grin never faltered, but her eyes hardened.

"What exactly do you want?"

"I want my friend or I go to the police."

Muriel's face softened into a pitiful stare.

"Oh I'm so sorry, my dear, but that little trollop is already dissolving in the tub. It does take a while for the acid to corrode the bones, though. I'm sure I could fish some out for you. How would that be?"

Cheryl ground her teeth. "You're lying."

"You're welcome to go check for yourself."

Cheryl pulled her hands from her pockets and flicked open the blade. She yanked on the screen door and flashed the knife in the woman's face.

"Then I want money."

"Now where would an old lady like me come up with enough money to buy your silence?"

Cher almost slashed the woman's throat right there. The thin sheen of sweat glistening on Muriel's brow, however, made her pause. The old woman was afraid. She was good at hiding it, but not that good. Maybe Cher would have a little fun with the old bird before she made the deal. She shoved her way into the foyer then closed and locked the door behind her.

Cheryl held the knife in Muriel's face, taking small satisfaction in watching the woman squirm. She glanced around the small living room to the right.

"I know your husband retired with a hefty pension from GM and when he died, his insurance policy was rather handsome. So don't give me any shit about how you're just a poor old widow, okay?"

Anger flared in Muriel's eyes. "Fine. What do you want to do?"

"Well, for one, you're going to head over to your bank and withdraw me a big pile of cash. Today. Then you're going to meet me out at the old Baker place outside of town and hand it over. My friend is already there waiting. If neither of us shows up, she's calling the cops."

"Well, I don't drive. How am I-?"

Forever Trapped

"Oh, so that old station wagon in the driveway just sits there unused all day?"

Muriel pursed her lips as Cher grinned.

"That's what I thought. Before you head out, though, maybe I'll just take a look around to see if anything else here tickles my fancy."

"So not only are you going to rob me of my life's savings, but you're going to take my precious belongings, too?"

"I'm not sure. Most of this stuff looks like junk to me."

Muriel glanced at her bedroom door. Cher caught the fear in her eyes when she did. The old lady tried to pretend she hadn't done it, but it was too late. Cheryl figured there must be some treasures in that room. Jewels stuffed in the old bat's panty drawer, cash in the mattress. Cher grinned.

"What's in there, Mrs. Spencer? Something you don't want me to find, I'll bet."

"No. There's nothing in there. Just a spare room I use for storing things. Photo albums, old clothes. Really."

"Uh huh. Step aside."

Cher gave the old woman a shove as she moved past her toward the bedroom. She gripped the old glass doorknob and turned it. Pushing the door open, she took a quick survey of its contents: dresser to the left, nightstand right by the bed, closet in the far corner...

What the hell? Someone was in the bed. She stepped closer to get a better look. At first she thought it was some old man sleeping, as if Muriel had a lover or something. But as the details became clearer, she realized her mistake.

Cher had come here thinking she could bully the old woman into giving her everything she wanted. And if she refused, she had no problems calling the cops to have the old bat arrested, even if meant getting in trouble herself. What she hadn't counted on was the level of pure evil residing in this house. The old woman's husband, dead for some years now, was lying in a mummified state in her bedroom. She probably sat beside him every night, telling him all about her day: the gardening, what mail was brought, whom she'd tied up and tortured, and whom she killed. Cheryl could picture her kissing him goodnight before lying down to sleep beside him every evening.

Before she could chastise herself for not thinking of this possibility sooner, the old woman grabbed her from behind. Cheryl could only watch as the straight razor's blade flashed in front of her face. She felt its cold hardness against her throat as it sliced through her flesh. The last thing she saw was the short shag of rose-colored carpet as she hit the floor. The last thing she heard was the old woman's laughter.

Muriel stood over the young woman's body and chuckled. The arrogance of youth. That was why she, or she and Harold, could take any of them down. The young always underestimated the old. She watched as the blood pumped out of Cheryl's body. Tsking aloud, she shuffled as quickly as she could to the kitchen to get a garbage bag. She needed wrap the girl's head and neck in the plastic to keep as much blood off the carpet as possible. Blood was so difficult to get out of any fabric. The less scrubbing she had to do, the better.

After wrapping the girl up, she dragged her through the kitchen and toward the basement steps. There was a disadvantage of being old – she wasn't strong enough to carry the body downstairs. So once she reached the steps, she pushed the corpse and let gravity do all the work. Once it was down, she dragged it into the middle of the floor. She'd leave it here for now and take care of it later. Once she met up with the friend and disposed of her, she could come back home and get rid of this little hooligan.

A quiet whimpering caught her attention and she looked toward the young woman still tied up in the chair. Yes, she had lied about this one already being dead. It was thrilling to know that the whore would sit there all day and watch over her friend's corpse. Muriel decided to let her watch one more friend get the tub treatment before killing her. Besides, she didn't have the strength to kill three people in one day. That would be too much for her old bones, no matter how tempting.

Back upstairs, Muriel grabbed her oversized handbag and threw in a small flashlight, the straight razor she used on Cheryl, a length of rope, and a few syringes filled with sedatives. She pinned a pillbox hat onto her head and headed out to the driveway. Nearsightedness was her only malady so she was able to maintain a valid license year after year.

She cranked the station wagon's engine and headed out to the old Baker home. She'd be able to drive out there, take care of this friend, and be home before supper. The home was abandoned so leaving the body there to rot wouldn't be a big issue, and easier on her back. If it ever was found, it would just be another unsolved murder for the police files.

Muriel pulled the car off to the side of the road about a mile from the home and killed the engine. She pulled the straight razor from her purse and slipped it into one of her coat pockets for easy access. She shuffled toward the house and made her way to the front porch. The dead grass and trees around the home gave her the willies. The complete absence of sound made her shudder in fear. *I guess there are still things in this life that can scare me*, she thought.

She climbed the steps to the porch, each one creaking in the silence swaddling the house. Muriel looked around, feeling as if eyes were upon her. She shook off that feeling and stepped up to the front door. Muriel wasn't sure if this friend would be ready to jump her the second she entered or was hiding in the shadows. She gripped the razor in her pocket just in case she needed to use it fast.

Pulling open the screen, the thought of the front door being locked flew through her mind. But before she could think of an alternate plan to enter the home, the door opened easily under her hand. She grinned, her fear forgotten. She called out to the darkness.

"Hello? Anyone here?"

A mysterious shape brushed past her and slammed the door closed, leaving Muriel alone in the darkness. But not for long.

Two police officers stood next to the empty station wagon. Someone had called the night before saying Mrs. Spencer had left her home early in the afternoon, but never returned. They were worried the car may have broken down, leaving her stranded and helpless somewhere.

Just after sunset, Office Gerald called in to say he'd found an abandoned station wagon matching the description of the missing vehicle. Officer Reynolds drove out to meet him.

Forever Trapped

Within ten minutes, they stood by the car discussing the possibilities.

"Doesn't look like there's any forced entry or sign of a struggle."

Gerald nodded in agreement. "I've searched the surrounding area, but there's no sign of her. I'm wondering if her car broke down and someone came along to help her out."

"More than likely. The closest house is the old Baker place, but that would have been too far for her to walk. From what her neighbors said, she's a frail old lady and barely capable of tending the little garden at her home."

"I hate to say it, but I wonder if someone attacked her. There's no sign of any vehicles past this point. I bet someone drove up, saw a helpless old woman that they could take advantage of, and promised to give her a ride back into town. Once they turned around, they would have been able to take her wherever they wanted. Then they could've dumped her body and no one would be the wiser."

Officer Reynolds shook his head. "What is this world coming to?"

PETER AND SALLY CONNERS
(1954)

Peter stood over the boy with his booted foot pressing into the youngster's neck. Sally giggled as she entwined her fingers with Peter's and stared at the terrified kid. As Peter shifted more of his weight forward, the boy finally lost consciousness. A dark wet stain spread across the front of his pants. Sally squealed.

"Yes! You did it, Peter!"

Peter whooped in triumph and lifted his boot. He knelt down next to boy and pressed an ear to his chest. A frail flutter *thump-thumped* behind the ribcage, but its pace steadied in moments. Peter smirked.

"Well, the rodent is still alive."

"Shoot. What do you think'll happen when he comes to?"

Peter chuckled. "He'll run home like a good little spaz."

"What if he tells his parents?"

"How do you think he got himself in this predicament today? If he's not as dumb as he looks, he'll keep this nice and quiet."

Sally giggled again and kissed Peter on the cheek. "God, I love it when you're all manly and confident like this."

Peter grabbed her by the waist and pulled her close. He clamped his mouth over hers and they shared a long deep kiss. As they pulled apart, Peter scanned the empty lot and surrounding area.

"Just to be safe, let's get the hell out of here before someone shows up."

Sally nodded and untangled herself from Peter. They jogged a few blocks away from the unconscious boy. Once they neared the center of town they walked, taking on the air of a casual stroll, pretending to window shop as they passed the drug store, pet shop, and shoe store. After they passed the hardware store, they took a left down Main Street. At Worthington, they took another left and in two blocks, turned into the driveway of a small frame home.

Peter led the way up the front steps and pushed through the door.

"Mom? We're home."

"In here, kids."

Peter and Sally dropped their schoolbooks onto the living room sofa and headed into the kitchen, following the sound of their mother's voice. The smell of chocolate chip cookies wafted over them as they made their way through the house. Peter snatched one off a large tray on the kitchen table then took a large bite and walked over to his mother. He gave her a gentle kiss on the cheek as she stood at the sink peeling potatoes.

"Hello, son."

"Hey, Mom. Great cookies."

"Thank you, sweetheart."

He grinned through a mush of chocolate and dough then turned to the fridge to get some milk. Sally skipped the cookies and walked straight to her mother, also kissing her on the cheek.

"Hi, Mom."

"Hello, darling. How was school?"

"Oh, same as it is every day. You know, boring."

She shared a secret smile with her brother. He winked at her over his glass of milk.

"That's right, Mom. Nothing exciting ever happens at school."

"Oh, now you two must be pulling my leg. I bet you get into all sorts of shenanigans. That's what high school is all about, after all."

Peter nearly choked on his beverage. Sally giggled and wrapped her arm around her mother's slim shoulders.

"Now, Mother. How can you say that? You know that Peter and I are straight as arrows. We get all A's, he's on the track team, and I'm a cheerleader. What more could you possibly want in such perfect children?"

"Oh, you silly girl. You stop teasing your poor mother."

Sally kissed her again and went back to get her books.

"I've got some Biology homework to do so I'll be in my room if anyone wants me."

She stared at Peter as she emphasized the word "wants". He licked his lips then pursed them at her. He grabbed two more cookies off the plate and went to get his books as well.

"I've got homework, too. So I'll be in *my* room."

"All right, dear. Dinner will be ready at six."

Peter and Sally's mother dropped the potato peeler into the sink as her shoulders shook. She wept silently over the brown strips in front of her. After a few minutes she wiped her hands on her apron then across her face. She walked to the hall entrance and checked to see if the kids' bedroom doors were closed. Satisfied they wouldn't see her, she tiptoed to the bathroom and shut and locked the door.

Standing at the sink, she stared at her reflection in the mirror. A dark purple bruise cradled her right eye. She'd been careful not to turn her face toward her children as they greeted her. True, they would see it soon enough, but she wanted them to be able to enjoy as much of the day as they could and concentrate on their homework. They would see her latest injury given by their father soon enough.

She hated herself for being so weak, for staying in such a horrible and loveless marriage. But what else could she do? She couldn't provide for the children by herself; she had no skills and no idea of how to go about getting any. She was raised to believe that a woman's purpose was to become a wife and mother. Once she was both, there was no point in looking forward to anything else.

How was this affecting her children? she worried. Sure they were good kids. Just like Sally said, they were excellent students, popular and outgoing, but she worried that growing up in such a violent household might scar them in some way. She sighed and put a washcloth in the sink. As the cool water flowed over it, her shoulders sagged. She supposed she would just have to hope for the best.

She dabbed the cool damp cloth over her face. Feeling better, she wrung out the extra water then hung it over the edge of the tub to dry. She stared at her reflection again and smoothed down a few stray hairs that had come unpinned from the bun of hair at the back of her head. Forcing a smile, she headed back to the kitchen to finish preparing dinner.

As she walked down the hall, she heard a muffled thump come from Sally's room. She pressed her ear against the door, but heard nothing more. She knocked and called to her daughter.

"Sally? Is everything all right?"

"Of course, mother. I just knocked the lamp off my nightstand by accident. Uh, what time is dinner again?"

"Six o'clock. Are you sure you're all right?"

"Yes, Mother. I'm fine. I've got to get back to my homework. I'd like to be finished before we eat."

"All right. Let me know if you need anything."

"Thanks, Mom."

As their mother headed back to the kitchen, Sally slapped Peter on the shoulder.

"Damnit, Peter. You've got to be more careful!"

He pulled at the clasp on her bra, now exposed after slipping off her sweater.

"I'm sorry, Sal, but you just get me so worked up."

She smiled and pushed him onto his back on the bed. Straddling him, she reached behind her back and unhooked the bra with ease then held it up over her head. Peter reached up and cupped her breasts. As he massaged them, she dropped the bra onto the floor and leaned forward to kiss him.

By six-thirty that night, Sally, Peter, and their parents sat around the dinner table in their usual silence. Their father shoveled mashed potatoes and baked chicken into his mouth while their mother sipped at her water between small bites. Sally and Peter glared at their father, both ignoring the food before them. They hated when he acted as if nothing was wrong. For him, each day he beat their mother seemed no different than a day he hadn't.

Sally eyed the steak knife laying beside Peter's plate. She looked up at him, back down at the knife, and back to Peter. He nodded his understanding. She turned to her mother, who sat on her right, and placed a hand on her shoulder.

"Mom, are you all right? You look really tired."

Her mother looked up, confused, as if she heard a far-off distant voice calling her name.

"What? What was that, sweetheart?"

Sally's heart broke at the term of affection her mother uttered. Even from within her sad reverie, their mother never stopped loving her children. It hardened Sally's resolve. She glared at her father even as she spoke to her mom.

"I said you look tired. I think you worked too hard today. Why don't you take a valium and go lie down? Peter and I will take care of the dishes, all right?"

As she had hoped, her father pointed his cool consideration at both she and her mother. From the corner of her eye, Sally saw Peter slip the knife into the napkin in his lap. Their mother wiped a shaking hand across her cheek.

"Well, I do feel a bit run down this evening. Perhaps I will go to bed early tonight."

She patted her daughter's cheek. Sally's heart fractured again with pain for her mother.

"Thank you, dear. What would I do without you and Peter?"

Their father sniffed and returned to his meal. Peter stood as his mother got up from the table then nodded at Sally. As he walked with his mother to her room, Sally rose from her chair and slipped over into the seat her had mother vacated. She scooched the chair closer to her father and smiled as he glanced sideways at her. After he realized how close she sat to him, he turned to look at her.

As he did, Peter returned from escorting their mother to her room and pulled his chair up to their father's side, opposite Sally, and sat down. He then turned to face Peter, swallowing his mouthful of food. When he looked back at Sally, his eyebrows arched in curiosity. It wasn't a friendly expression, but it was his softest and least threatening.

"What exactly are you two doing?"

"Dad," Peter began, "I was just thinking. That is, Sally and I were thinking."

"Well, that's a first," their father replied.

Peter's jaw muscles bunched as he clenched his teeth. Sally shook her head, a small gesture that only Peter could see. As their father turned his attention back to his meal, Sally's lips curled into a sly smile. She reached up and ran her fingers through the salt and pepper wavy hair at his ear. He jerked away as if she had scratched him. His lip curled in disgust.

"What's the matter, Daddy? Don't you like me? Don't you like having your only daughter touch you?"

She stroked his hair again and when he leaned away, she reached up and yanked a fistful of it, pulling his head back. Without letting go, she stood and kicked her chair away. She straddled her father's lap and lowered her face down to his, brushing her lips against his mouth.

"What makes you so special? Peter loves it when I touch him, don't you Peter?"

Peter stood and walked behind their father so he could be face to face with Sally. He stroked her hair and kissed the top of her head.

"Oh, yes. More than anything."

Their father jerked underneath Sally's weight.

"What is wrong with you two? You disgust me. How could I ever have fathered such perverted and twisted children?"

Sally smiled and used her other hand to pull Peter closer. She kissed him deep and hard, gyrating against her father and pushing her breasts into his face. Her father muffled his protests into her cleavage, which made her pull away laughing.

"Daddy, that tickles!"

Peter laughed and smacked his father in the back of the head. He frowned and tried to twist around to glare at his son, but Sally grabbed his head and forced him to look at her. She dug her hips against his.

"You say *we're* twisted? That we're evil? You have no one to blame but yourself. You made us what we are."

She stopped gyrating her hips and ran her tongue across her bottom lip. She looked down at her father's lap then purred into his ear.

"Seems you like me more than you're letting on, Daddy."

His face flushed and he bucked against her. Peter pushed down on his shoulders, surprisingly strong for an 18-year old, and held their father in place. Sally and Peter smiled at each other over their father's head. As soon as he stopped fighting, Peter stepped back and held the steak knife at his side. Sally grinned and looked down at her father. He growled.

"I am not responsible for this perversion. I only taught you the virtue of righteous living through the Bible. And discipline is the only way to-"

"Oh, right. Of course. 'Spare the rod, spoil the child,', right, Dad?" Peter snickered into his ear. "It was bad enough how you treated us, but to apply your brilliant philosophy to mother as well? What did she ever do to deserve this hell except marry you?"

As their father fumed, Sally stroked his cheek.

"Don't worry, Daddy. You were very successful in teaching us lasting lessons from the Bible. Here's one that stands out for me."

She brushed her lips against his again and whispered into his mouth.

"For the day of vengeance is in mine heart, and the year of my redeemed is come."

She stood slowly and stepped back, looking down at her father's pinched and frightened face. She looked up at Peter and smiled. Peter pulled the knife back and plunged it through the opening in the back of the chair, piercing their father's lung. Unable to scream, he jerked in pain. Peter pulled the knife back then stabbed the other lung. He pulled the knife out and thrust it in his father's body over and over until he slumped forward and fell to the floor.

Peter stood behind the chair, calmly surveying the spreading pool of blood forming around the body. Sally kicked at it just to make sure he was dead. Peter walked to the kitchen sink and washed the blood from his hands and the knife. He grabbed a box of large black garbage bags from a low cupboard and dumped the contents. He handed one at a time to Sally, who laid them across the floor.

After creating a rectangle eight bags wide and five bags long, they rolled their father's body onto them and hoped the seeping blood would stay on the plastic. As their father lay there, getting colder each minute, the two of them cleaned the coagulating blood from the orange and yellow linoleum floor with several old towels and rags. When they had finished, Peter had an idea.

"All right. Here's what we do. Mother will be passed out for the rest of the night. We'll clean out dad's clothes and belongings, pack them in his suitcase, and dump them and his body where no one will find them. Everyone will think he just up and left."

"Sounds good to me. But we can't let anyone see us driving his car."

"Hmmm. You're right about that. I'll put on some of his clothes. People say I look like him anyway. If anyone is

Forever Trapped

watching, they'll think I'm him. You can duck down in the back seat where no one will see you."

Sally smiled. "Perfect."

She leaned into him and gave him a kiss then ran down into the basement and returned with a roll of silver duct tape. Peter frowned in confusion. She held it up.

"We can't just roll dad up in the dining room rug. Mom will notice if that goes missing. We'll tape him up in the plastic bags. She won't realize if some tape and garbage bags are missing."

Peter winked at her and took the tape from her hand. Over the next twenty minutes they wrapped plastic and tape around their father's body. Once he was bundled into a neat cocoon, Peter and Sally snuck into their parents' room to gather their father's belongings. Their mother snored under the blanket of modern pharmaceuticals and never stirred at their intrusion.

Within the hour they had the car packed with their father's body and suitcase. Peter sat behind the wheel dressed in one of his father's dark suits and overcoat. Sally stretched out onto the back seat of the car. She gently pushed against the back of the driver's seat to get Peter's attention.

"Where are we going to take him?"

"I was thinking out behind that abandoned house by the cliffs. No one goes out there anymore and the house has been empty for years. I guess nobody wants to buy it. Even the toughs who go out to the rocks to drink and smoke won't go near the property. We can bury Dad and his stuff in the backyard."

"Why don't we just throw him over the cliff into the sea?"

"We can't risk his body washing up somewhere down the shore. We don't want anyone to find him ever."

Sally nodded. "That makes sense. All right. Let's get this over with."

"Well, we don't have to rush back. Mother will be out for the rest of the night and no one knows what we're doing or where we're going. Why don't we check out the old house while we're there?"

Sally's jaw dropped and she popped up from the back seat. "Are you nuts? Why would you want to do that?"

"Oh, come on," Peter turned to look back at her. "Don't tell me you've never thought of exploring that old place."

Sally tried to grimace, but found herself smiling instead.

"Okay. Yes, I have. What do you think it's like inside? Do you think all the original furniture is in there? How old is that place again? It must be so ancient. We could get into *all kinds* of trouble in there."

She reached over the back of the seat and stroked her fingers over her father's crisp white shirt that Peter wore. He laughed and gripped her hand. "I don't know. I don't know. I'm not sure, but probably really really ancient. And I sure hope so."

She giggled and ducked back down behind the seat. He started the car, pulled out of the attached garage and onto the road. As he drove down the street, he and Sally shared a light-hearted laugh, thinking of all the fun they could have in that old house.

SYLVIA MATHESON
(1984)

She jumped back when the chief medical examiner unzipped the body bag. Not from the smell of the corpse, but because of its condition. In the past five years of working in the morgue at County Hospital, Sylvia had never seen this type of mutilation. Anyone would think she had, but this wasn't Baltimore or Detroit. This city just didn't have the same type of sickos hanging around. But now it seemed some kind of local wacko had moved into her quiet suburban town.

The woman on the table was approximately twenty-five years old, thin but athletic, wavy blonde hair, and rather pretty. Or she would have been if someone hadn't ripped strips of skin from her face and neck or removed both her eyes and filled the empty sockets with broken glass. Sylvia covered her mouth trying to hold back a surge of vomit. Jay Murphy, the CME, shook his head.

"Holy shit. What the hell?"

Apparently Jay had never seen anything like this either. Though he was able to keep his cool and hold down his breakfast, his expression told the truth of his feelings. He drew the blunt end of his scalpel alongside one of the edges of the raw exposed flesh on the woman's neck. Leaning over her face, Jay eased a shard of glass from one of her eye sockets. He held it up to the light.

"Christ on His cross. What will come through here next?"

Sylvia didn't want to know. And hoped never to find out. Unfortunately, she'd have to encounter similar acts of cruelty and psycho mutilation several more times over the coming months. None of the bodies that came through like this woman were ever thought to be connected. They had no similar friends or families, job, or hobbies. Hell, they weren't even all women. The only thing they had in common was the horrific manner of their deaths.

She worked on six bodies that arrived in this state. Most of the time she saw the usual fare: car accidents, overdoses, firearm disputes (the ones where the corpse brought in had an argument with their pistol and lost), a few suicides. But even though the ghastly murders were few in number, they were disturbing and Sylvia had a hard time shaking them from her memory. How could anyone forget a woman who had been dismembered only to have her parts sewn crudely back onto her body in all the wrong places? Or the man who was given a sex change, probably not by choice, while still in his three-hundred-dollar wool suit?

After the sixth victim was brought in, Sylvia had trouble finding the desire to come into work each day. She had volunteered to assist Jay in the morgue until they hired a new assistant. Her section in the Nephrology department had been overstaffed and the hospital offered plump bonuses for anyone willing to help out down here. Now she wondered if her supportive attitude would be her undoing.

As the weeks turned into months, she dreaded the possibility that another mutilated body might be waiting for her and Jay when they arrived at work. She'd already used up most of her sick days over this, though. Soon, her boss would think she was a total basket case and fire her. Or think she was incapable of doing her job. Another scenario that would only end with her termination.

Pushing her way through the morgue doors, she took a deep breath to calm her nerves. Please, God, don't let me find some poor soul with his head literally shoved up his ass. Jay already stood over a body and turned when she entered the room. He noted the anxious look on her face and smiled.

"Don't worry. No creative deaths this morning. Not that this one isn't interesting, but I don't think some psycho got a hold of him."

Sylvia pulled on some rubber gloves and moved next to Jay. She looked down at the table to see a man lying face down with a gigantic hole in the back of his head. She frowned, her fears gone as her professional instincts took over.

"Doesn't look like a gun shot. What happened?"

"The report just said that he was found in an abandoned underground parking lot, face down, with his pants around his ankles. And there was a twelve-inch metal spike next to his body."

"A spike?"

"Yeah, I know. Probably not the most common choice for a murder weapon. Seeing as this man was found in a place well known for its illicit activities, it's not that unusual to find all sorts of people killed by odd means. Poor schmuck. I'd hate to have been the officer that had to tell his family about this."

Sylvia grabbed the file on the counter and flipped it open. Charles Daley, aged forty, married with two children. Sylvia felt the blood drain from her face.

"Holy crap, I know this guy. He's a friend of my brother's."

"Eeesh. Sorry."

As Sylvia nodded her head, her pager beeped. She laid down the file and held the little black box up to her face. Carl's number flashed across the display and she forgot all about the dead man. She smiled and turned to Jay, who was already shooing her out the door.

"Go on and talk to your stud. This is our only case so far today and I think we can rule out accidental death."

Sylvia pinched Jay's cheek and skipped out the door. She jogged to the elevators and punched the button for the fourth floor. Carl Bookman was the head of Pediatrics at County Hospital and Sylvia had been dating him for a year. As a matter of fact, today was their one-year anniversary and they had planned a romantic dinner for later.

She strolled down the hallway to his office and tapped on the door. He called for her to enter and she pushed her way in, smiling. Her smile faltered as she looked at him.

"Everything okay, Carl?"

"No, Sylvia. It's not. That's why I paged you. Please, sit down."

She didn't like the tone of his voice. Whenever something was wrong with a patient, his voice took on a soft but condescending tone. That's what he sounded like now. She lowered herself into one of the plush chairs across from him and tensed.

"What's going on?"

He took a slow deep breath then pushed the air out through tight lips. "This isn't easy for me to say so I'm just going to be blunt. I don't think we should see each other anymore."

Sylvia's mouth twitched in a half smile. Whenever she got bad news, her first reaction was to smile, as if someone was playing a joke and couldn't possibly be telling the truth.

"What?"

"I said I don't think we-"

"I heard you, Carl. I just, well, I can't believe it. Why?"

"I just think that we've grown apart. We're not really compatible anymore."

Sylvia blinked and shook her head. Didn't he just say last week that their upcoming anniversary was so important because it marked a great milestone in their relationship? What the hell? Then it hit her and her disbelief turned to anger.

"You're seeing someone else, aren't you?"

"Oh come on, Sylvia. That's not what's happening here. We just want different things now."

"Who is she?"

"Sylvia," Carl tried to reason with her.

"Carl, either you tell me who she is or I start ripping appendages."

He sighed. "Madeleine Harper."

Sylvia racked her brain. Did that name mean anything? Did she know this Madeline? Then an image of the twenty-two-year-old secretary from Administration with the fake boobs and plastic Barbie wanna-be look flashed through her mind. She leaped to her feet as rage surged through her body.

"Madeleine? That, that *skank* from the admin office? You can't be serious. What could the two of you possibly have in common other than the obvious need to fuck me over?"

"Sylvia, please. You're acting like a child."

She gaped at him. He actually had the gall to turn this on her. He rose from his chair and stepped around his desk.

"You had to know this was coming. I mean, really. Did you honestly think I was going to spend the rest of my life with an RN-slash-morgue attendant? I'm the head of Pediatrics. How would that look?"

She cocked her right arm and slugged him with all of her might. His head snapped back and he went down like a bag of rocks. Already she could see the bruise forming along his jaw at the 'sweet spot', the bundle of nerves that when hit, caused instant unconsciousness, exactly where her boxing coach said it was. She smirked down at his prone body, whipped her head around as she turned, and stormed out of his office.

By the time she got to the elevators, some of the steam from her anger dissipated. She stood, defeated, as she waited for the elevator to arrive. Her eyes welled up with tears, but she refused to cry over this. She didn't want to give Carl the satisfaction of knowing that he had broken her heart.

When the doors opened, her friend, Connie, the head nurse in the cardiac department, stood in the car. She looked up and smiled when she saw Sylvia. Sylvia's mouth twitched in greeting and Connie stepped forward.

"Sylvia, are you okay?"

Sylvia shook her head. She couldn't find her voice to answer. A single tear rolled down her cheek. Great. So much for her whole 'not-crying' plan. Connie put her arm around Sylvia's shoulders and ushered her into the elevator. She glanced down the hallway toward Carl's office and realized that Sylvia had just been dumped.

"It's all right, hon. You just come with me. I've got a five-pound box of chocolates in my office that'll satisfy you more than that jerk ever could."

A week later, Sylvia was sitting in St. Thomas church for Charles Daley's funeral. God, she hated these things. Maybe if she'd known the man better, she'd feel more sympathy for his family. But he was her brother's friend, and he had asked her to come, so she obliged. Her brother kept blathering about something while they waited for the service to begin. He was always nervous at funerals and felt the constant need for noise and chatter until he could calm down. She picked up the hymnal in front of her and toyed with the pages, looking around at the beautiful details of the church architecture. Too bad she didn't give a crap about any of it.

Her gaze fell to the people in the pews around her and just as she blew a lock of hair from her forehead, she locked eyes with the man across the aisle. Heat rushed up her neck. She was embarrassed to be caught in an act of obvious boredom, but he only smiled, as if in camaraderie. His dark hair framed a strong angular jaw, straight nose, and dark eyes. She wondered if the rest of him looked as good under that suit.

The priest stood up on the altar and began the service. She whipped her head forward, mentally chastising herself for stripping a man naked in her thoughts while in a church. At a funeral, no less. But throughout the service, she kept sneaking glances of him and caught him looking at her as well.

Once the service ended, she lurched out of the pew to head outside for a smoke. Maybe she'd get a chance to chat with the cute guy who had sat across from her. When she got through the doors, she searched her purse for her cigarettes only to find the empty pack she had finished the previous night. Cursing under her breath, she looked up to see the good-looking guy standing off to the side, staring at her. Smiling, she walked over to him and pointed at his cigarette.

"I don't suppose you've got one of those to spare, do you?"

He held out his pack and she grabbed two, putting one behind her ear for later. She looked up as he flipped open a Zippo lighter. His lips twisted in a small smile as he motioned at the cigarette behind her ear. She pointed at it as she fumbled an excuse.

"Ah. You know, cigarettes are kinda like potato chips. You can't have just one. So instead of bothering you twice to bum one, I just figured I'd get it over with and take two right from the get-go."

"I see. Makes sense."

She mentally slapped herself. God she could be such a dork sometimes. He smiled, though, so she hadn't turned him off yet. He didn't say anything else, however, only lit another cigarette. Great, he thinks I'm an idiot. Well, no point in opening my mouth to solidify that sentiment. She took a deep drag from the cigarette and hoped he would be discreet about walking away and leaving her standing alone and humiliated. He surprised her instead.

"I'm Daniel, by the way. Your cigarette supplier for this trip."

She laughed and introduced herself. They had a nice quick conversation before deciding to blow off the brunch and have coffee elsewhere so they could get to know each other better. She tracked down her brother to let him know she didn't need a ride home and would see him later. He looked over her shoulder at Daniel and nudged her in the ribs. She slapped his arm then walked off with Daniel.

Several weeks later Sylvia sat in the break room at the hospital with Connie. She was gushing over Daniel for the umpteenth time, but to her friend's credit, Connie never complained. She was probably relieved that Sylvia wasn't moping anymore.

"The only thing is," Sylvia began then paused.

"What is it? Is he too big? Maybe a little to rough with playtime? Or is he not rough enough?" Connie's eyes twinkled.

"I wouldn't know."

Connie frowned. "What do you mean, you wouldn't know? You are sleeping with him, aren't you?"

"No, I'm not. That's the problem," Sylvia said. "We make out and have great grope-fests, but if it starts to get too heavy, he backs off and takes me home."

"Oh, Lord. He's gay."

Sylvia burst out laughing. "He's not gay, Connie. Well, I'm pretty sure he's not gay. He couldn't be gay. Could he?"

Connie just raised her eyebrows and lowered her chin. Sylvia chewed on her bottom lip.

"We've got a date tonight so I'll find out what the hell is going on. I'll just come right out and ask him. Really, I will."

"Mmm-hmm. You just let me know how that goes for you, okay?"

Sylvia swiped at Connie as she dodged away. That's just what I'll do, Sylvia thought. I'm going to get to the bottom of this tonight. And then maybe I can get to his bottom.

She confronted Daniel in his car as they were making out, again, after their date. She was so terrified that he would say he *was* gay that she figured any other excuse he made would be acceptable, and they could work around it. When he told her that he was worried about hurting her, she almost jumped out of her skin right there. After Carl, it was such a relief and a wonder to hear from a man who worried about her feelings.

She convinced him that she was a big girl and could take care of herself. For crying out loud, she was practically raping him in the backseat of his car. And, even more to her surprise, he wanted to make sure their first time was something special, not just a drag out sweating marathon of great (she hoped) sex like a couple of high school virgins.

As he drove down a rough dirt road toward his home in a secluded neighborhood, she eyed a monstrosity of a house on their left. She shuddered as goose bumps popped up all over her skin. She looked at it one more time over her shoulder as they drove past it. Who in their right mind would ever want to go into that house?

After another ten minutes, Daniel pulled the car into the driveway of a small cozy ranch-style house. The grass looked a little worse for wear, but she understood how a busy work schedule could keep him from staying on top of the yard work. It was unusual, though, for a single man to live in something so quaint. She told him as much, so when he thought that meant she didn't want to go in, she grabbed his hand and pulled him up to the small porch.

He opened the front door and ushered her inside. The moment she stepped over the threshold, she knew something was wrong. She couldn't put her finger on it right away. It took her brain several minutes to realize that the few pieces of furniture in the house were draped with sheets. A thin film of dust covered the small ledge on her right. No one lived here, least of all a top advertising executive.

"What?" she began to say. He grinned and made a comment about the cleaning lady having the week off.

"What's going on here, Daniel? Is this some kind of joke?"

"No, not really. Well, not a joke on me, anyway."

As that truth sunk in, she realized this wasn't going to be a night filled with sensual lovemaking or even plain, old, hot sex. She was going to die here. By his casual demeanor and his flippant conversation, she wasn't his first either. He'd killed before. And not just a handful of times, but more like dozens. How could she have been so stupid? She was supposed to be this strong modern woman. She had smarts, a good job, and a decent body. Was she so desperate for a man to love her that she didn't see the warning signs? Had her gut been screaming at her to see him for what he was, but she couldn't hear it because her groin was screaming louder?

She looked around for any kind of weapon, but the home was barren. He knew what she was thinking and gloated in the fact that she was helpless here. Bullshit, she thought. Sylvia tried to remember her boxing training and prepared herself for a fight. She'd rather run like hell, but he stood between her and the door.

He threw a few punches at her, which she dodged. It wasn't until he commented on how happy he was that she was giving him a run for his money that she brought the fight to him. She swung her purse up and around and caught him in the side of the face. She was aiming for his eyes and was lucky enough to have found her mark. He fell to one knee and she wasted no time in kicking him while he was down.

She rammed her heel into his exposed knee and he howled. When he fell over she ran for the door. Snapping the locks out of place, she threw the door open and fled out into the night. She looked back once and saw him on his feet. Pumping her arms harder, she tried to put as much distance between them as possible.

When she got to the open road, she couldn't gain much distance. These fucking high heels. Why the hell did she wear them? *Because they make your legs look fantabulous, you dipshit. Now stop thinking about your god damned shoes and figure out how to get yourself out of this mess.* Then his voice echoed through the dark as he called her name.

As she turned to see how far behind he was, she stumbled. She crashed face down onto the dirt and gravel, scraping her left leg and cracking her knee on a large rock. She struggled to get back up, then started to run again. Pain flared up and down her leg. Sylvia bit back a scream as she hobbled down the road. She'd never make it back to town at this rate. He'd be on her in minutes and she'd be dead shortly thereafter. She glanced up to the right and saw the huge, abandoned home they had passed earlier that evening.

It was a long shot, but maybe she could find something in there to help her. Not a phone perhaps, but there could be something to use as a weapon against him. Hell, at the very least she could hide from him in that huge house long enough to rest her leg. Then she could sneak out and tear ass for town to get help.

She turned toward the home and rambled up a small hill. The dead, dry grass crackled under her feet. She lurched up the steps and launched herself at the front door. Sylvia worried that it might be locked and she wouldn't be able to get inside in time. But the door gave way under her weight as she turned the knob. After a millisecond of thinking how odd it was that the door was unlocked, she slammed it closed just as Daniel reached it.

Running into the living room on her right, a tiny vestige of hope surged, allowing her to think she might find a working phone. No phone in sight, of course. She hadn't really expected to find one, but even now it seemed she was still an optimist. She turned to look back at the foyer and thought she saw someone, a young girl. That couldn't be right. Rubbing her eyes, Sylvia thought that her vision hadn't adjusted to the gloom. When she looked again, the girl's form seemed more distinct. Several dark shapes spun around her.

Sylvia heard Daniel as he threw himself against the front door and crashed into the foyer. He rolled onto the floor, but was on his feet in seconds, laughing as he brushed dirt from his suit. He said something about how impressed he was with her, but she wasn't listening. When he realized she was looking past him, he turned to look into the other room.

He saw the girl too, she was sure of it. As he stared, more and more of the dark shapes swirled into view. They twisted and turned around the young girl as she moved forward. Daniel backed away and bumped into Sylvia. He seemed surprised by her presence, but grateful for it all the same. She clutched his arm, no longer worried about whether or not he was going to kill her. Sylvia knew that both of them were doomed.

JONATHAN CRANE
(1695)

"Not since Salem have I encountered such a foul temptress of a witch. Thou must end, beast."

Pastor Crane pulled the scythe high above his shoulder. He arced it down and sliced the woman's head neatly from her neck. Her long copper curls floated around her face as her head sailed through the air, up and away from her body. It rolled to a stop several yards away, the eyes frozen open in defiance. Her body slumped against the ropes that tied it to the wooden post. Blood seeped from the stump of her neck, coloring the front of her white nightshift with crimson stains.

The pastor stood back to study his work. He planted the scythe in the ground and leaned against it. His breath came in heavy gasps. No matter how his body may suffer from this work, his soul felt light. He could sleep well each night knowing that what he did was all for His glory.

This latest demon had been felled after a long and arduous fight. He'd run through many of his cleansing rituals, but she would not confess. She had not been deterred even after he had dispensed of the man foolish and lost enough to call himself her husband. That was when he knew only death would release this poor soul into the next world. As he stood before her with the scythe in hand, she pushed her chin forward in contempt. He knew God demanded her sacrifice for the benefit of all.

After laying the scythe at the dead woman's feet, Pastor Crane walked back into the church. The council of elders for the town of Everett sat in the pews in front of the altar. They turned in unison as the pastor entered, their faces revealing the fear in their hearts. The pastor nodded to them.

"It is done."

The council sighed as one, in relief and resignation. As much as they feared that the witch infestation was real, they were glad to have the services of Pastor Crane to cleanse their community. The head elder, Samuel Brown, stood and extended his hand.

"I cannot thank thee enough for thy holy service, Pastor Crane. I feared our town folk would be lost forever to Satan and his minions."

The Pastor stared at the offered hand, but did not shake it. "It is true that this evil has been cast out. But do not believe for one moment that this town is free from the devil's dark influence."

Samuel's face sagged. "Dost thou mean to say that Satan is still among us?"

"I do."

The council elders mumbled amongst themselves in fevered tones. Samuel once again approached the pastor.

"What must we do?"

"Allow me to continue the good Lord's work. I will weed out the evil from this town."

Over the next several weeks, Pastor Crane purged the evil in residence: Goody Adams, Mr. and Mrs. Carpenter, along with their three children, the widow Garner and her daughter-in-law, Sarah, the entire Baker family – John, Martha, and all six of their children, from Adam, the oldest at seventeen to Christina, the youngest at four, several council elders, including Samuel Brown, and all household pets, as Satan used these witches' familiars to spread the foul seeds of his darkness.

Soon the entire town of Everett lived in fear. Not of Satan, but of Pastor Crane. His religious fervor, heated by his passion for God, was only outdone by his fiery hatred of Satan. No one was safe from his wrath. The townsfolk kept their hearts and minds clean and their deeds pure to save their souls, and bodies, from Pastor Crane's inquisition.

One cold crisp afternoon, as the anguished screams of Pastor Crane's latest sinner echoed through the town, the remaining council elders met in secret in Caleb Pope's home to discuss a course of action. They could no longer sit back and watch as Pastor Crane systematically eliminated every last living creature unfortunate enough to cross his path.

"But, Caleb, what are we to do? Those who do not live in fear are in awe of him. No one will help us," John Goodwell pleaded.

"I do not know, but we must act, John. We must find a way to free ourselves from Pastor Crane's madness. Even if it is only we four who accomplish the task."

Robert Chase, Daniel Harwell, and John all nodded in agreement. Robert's eyes widened as he thought of something they could do. He looked to the others.

"I believe I know of a way."

Caleb leaned toward him, eager to listen. "What is it, Robert?"

"We shall take him to Tamesin's home."

Caleb stared at him. When he looked at Daniel and John, the fear and shame Caleb felt was mirrored in their faces. They knew it was the only way to stop Pastor Crane, but could they live with themselves if they went through with it?

"Robert, thou speaks blasphemy," Daniel chastised, but with little animation.

John nodded in agreement, but stared at the floor.

"How can we call ourselves righteous and moral if we condemn our fellow man to such damnation?"

"I fear we have no other choice," Caleb spoke. "If any here fear for thy souls in this endeavor, no one will judge if thou wishes to leave now, never to turn back."

All four men studied each other.

"I will not live in fear," Daniel said. "I will help."

"As will I," added John.

Caleb nodded. "I give all of thee my thanks. Now we must devise a plan to lure Pastor Crane to the home."

The following morning, Caleb made his way to the church, knowing Pastor Crane would be there, as he was every morning, performing his daily cleansing ritual. It seemed even Pastor Crane was not free from Pastor Crane's judgments.

Jonathan Crane knelt in front of the altar, his head bowed and his right arm trembling as he grasped the leather whip. His back was bathed in a mixture of sweat and fresh blood. Raw open wounds oozed across the older scars that crisscrossed his flesh.

As he stood at the back of the church, Caleb cleared his throat, but the pastor didn't hear him. After only a minute of rest, Pastor Crane lifted the whip and continued his ritual of self-flagellation. He grunted with each lashing. Caleb would have to approach him in order to make his presence known.

He stepped up behind the pastor and reached forward to get his attention. As he did, Pastor Crane shifted his weight and threw the whip over his left shoulder, catching Caleb's hand under its straps. A line of flesh ripped away and Caleb yelped as he jerked backwards. Pastor Crane snapped his head around and Caleb could see the fire of insanity burning in the man's eyes.

Pastor Crane looked down at Caleb's hand and his mouth curved into a small smirk.

"A small sacrifice of flesh and blood can do so much for the soul."

Caleb grimaced and cradled his hand. He took a step away from Pastor Crane lest the man feel the need for Caleb to sacrifice any more.

"Forgive me for interrupting, but my conscience would allow me no further delay."

The pastor's eyes widened. He stood, his six-foot two-inch frame towered over Caleb and glistened with slick fluids. He almost seemed to salivate at the prospect of Caleb bringing him news of new evil to fight. Caleb shivered at the sound of his name on the pastor's tongue.

"Tell me all thou knows, Caleb."

John, Daniel, Robert, and Caleb stood behind Pastor Crane as he surveyed the empty home. He squinted against the morning sun as Caleb explained its history.

"Tamesin was a young girl who lived here with her parents until three years ago. Her mother and father were accused and tried as witches. Both were hanged. The former pastor tried to save Tamesin, though it was clear she was just as much a witch as her family. She claimed her innocence to the last, but it did not save her from the noose. Before she died, she cursed this land, home, and all who were involved in her death. We believe," Caleb looked to the other men and they nodded for him to continue.

"We believe her spirit lingers in the home. It is possible her evil radiates through our town and that is why thou hast had to cleanse so many souls here. If thou destroys her, perhaps the town can be free."

Pastor Crane nodded. "That would explain the stain of evil that lives in this wretched town, Caleb. Why hast no one done anything about this foulness sooner?"

"I am ashamed to say no man, no person, possesses the courage to enter the home and rid us all of this evil."

A look of disgust washed over Pastor Crane's face as he studied each man behind him. He shook his head.

"It is no wonder the town of Everett is overrun by evil. With every day thou lacks action, Satan sends more of his minions to do his bidding. I am surprised this town still stands. Once

I dispense of this wicked plague, only God will know if thou are all truly free from sin."

The four men stepped away from him, but he only smiled. Pastor Crane turned back to the home. It was still in good shape, no unusual wear and tear that might come from a few years of neglect. That in itself surely made him suspicious that evil was alive and well in the house. But Caleb thought that the dead grass and trees surrounding the area solidified the pastor's conviction. Even Caleb believed nothing good and holy could cause this sort of palpable death.

Crane left the four men standing in fear behind him and approached the house. He marched up the steps and stood at the front door. Confident, he shouted to the spirit inside.

"Tamesin, thy foul spirit has no power here. God is thy master and He speaks through me. Thou will torment the living no longer. Go back to hell, witch!"

Pastor Crane strode through the front door, leaving it open as he stood in the entryway. Caleb, Daniel, Robert, and John watched from outside, each praying for forgiveness for their parts in this deception. Pastor Crane turned back, as if he wished to speak to them. Before he could make a sound, however, the door slammed shut. The four men gasped and stepped back, each making a sign of the cross.

When nothing more happened, Caleb turned to the others. He stared at each man and nodded his thanks. They headed back toward town, putting as much distance between themselves, the house, and Pastor Crane as quickly as they could. Caleb stopped and took one last look at the home. He thought he heard faint muffled screaming, but chalked it up to his imagination and turned back to catch up with the others.

PHIL HENDERSON
(MODERN DAY)

Phil approached the steps to the rehabilitation apartment building. He reached the top and checked himself. He smoothed his rumpled t-shirt, wishing the prescription codeine he took thirty minutes ago would hurry up and help quell the cocaine high he had right now. He'd been able to keep his addictions quiet while assuming the pretense of being clean and sober during his stay here for the past two years. It would be…inconvenient if Paula, the social worker on duty this afternoon, saw him buzzing. Lucky for him, Skinny Joe popped out from the alley to his right.

Skinny Joe showed up on the days he got his disability check and had money to burn. He stood at the alley opening, shaking, and rubbing his nose. His ragged clothes shifted with the breeze revealing smudges and stains of unknown substances. Clumps of matted brown hair perched in various spots on Skinny Joe's head, unaffected by the wind or his withdrawal vibrations. About the only things that didn't look worn or dirty on Joe were his eyes. Despite the years of abuse he inflicted on his body, his eyes were clear and bright, always on the lookout for the authorities or his next hit.

Phil sauntered over to the man and leaned against the dirty tan-bricked wall. He stood almost a foot taller than Joe, so he leaned down to be nose to nose with him. Probably not the best move since Skinny Joe smelled like rotten eggs, feces, and two-week old dirty gym socks, on a good day. Covering a grimace, he nudged Joe in the ribs.

"Nice day, ain't it, Joe?"

Skinny Joe gave Phil two quick and curt nods, his eyes darting back and forth between the street and the rehab doors.

"So what brings you here, SJ?"

The junkie finally looked up. Phil winced, not for the first time, as he looked into Joe's tortured eyes. *This is hell on two legs.* He understood what addiction could do to a man. He'd been through it himself, over and over, since he was fourteen. After floating through the system for the past twenty years, Phil had learned how to manipulate people, slip through the loopholes, and hide the truth. Now in his third stint of rehab, he knew all the tricks to keep his addictions fed without anyone finding out. He also learned how to enable other addicts to keep fighting their monkeys, riding their horses, and chasing their dragons.

"I need, I need…"

Phil patted Skinny Joe on the shoulder. "I know what you need, Joe. The question is do you have what I need?"

Joe dug into his right front pocket with a trembling hand. With a series of violent shakes, he gave Phil a crumpled piece of paper. Phil frowned and took it from him.

"What's this?"

"It's an, uh, an I.O.U. Please, Phil. I need it."

"Joe, you know I can't take this. It's real money or nothin'. Now do you have money on you today? You know, moooneeeey?"

Phil rubbed his fingers together in Joe's face to accent his point. Skinny Joe's brow creased in anxiety as he dug through all of his pockets. Besides a few balls of lint and a single penny, Joe had nothing to offer. He patted himself down again just in case there was a hidden roll of fifties stuck in the folds of his clothes, but Phil stopped him.

"Joe, stop. Stop. You know how it works. No money. No goods. It's the simple law of supply and demand."

Joe's eyes reflected the vacancy in the brainless void of his skull. The heroin he'd been steeping in his veins for the past ten years had destroyed all of his higher intellectual functions and left him with the simplistic but harsh ability to crave reality-altering drugs. He could only stare at Phil and fumble with the buttons on his shirt, helpless. Phil slapped him on the shoulder, nearly toppling the feeble man over.

"You just come see me when you got some money, okay, Joe?"

Phil didn't wait for a response. He turned and skipped up the front steps of the building, leaving Joe to stand swaying in the afternoon sun. Once in the darkened foyer, Phil squinted toward the back of the building. He could see the light from Paula's office, the main social worker on duty and his Case Manager in the rehab center. He smoothed down his hair as he walked down the hall. It was policy to check in with the office each time a patient came and went. He knocked on the door.

"C'mon in," Paula called to him.

Phil pushed open the office door and smiled down at Paula. She was a heavy-set woman in her mid fifties, wiry salt and pepper hair tied in a tight bun at the nape of her neck. The thick framed glasses she wore made her look like a giant bug, or a more feminine version of Harry Carey. She returned Phil's smile. He learned early on that he could charm the pants off Paula with little effort. So he put a tiny bit of extra oomph behind his smile today to distract her from his dilated pupils.

"Hey sweetness. Just wanted to let you know that I was back from the doc's. All is well. Arm's healing nicely."

"That's great to hear, Phil. Thanks for letting me know. Oh, Mark was looking for you. I think he's upstairs."

"Thanks, Paula. I'll catch you later."

Phil gave her a wink and a nod before closing the office door behind him. It was almost too easy.

The second floor of the rehab center consisted of several quads of rooms connected by a common area. Phil took the stairs two at a time. Mark was one of his roommates and he was probably looking to score a hit or two of the heroin Phil had tucked away in his front pocket. As he entered the quad, he heard a loud crash come from the back room, where Mark slept.

"Mark? Buddy, you back there?"

The door to Mark's room slammed open. The man who stood in the doorway looked half rabid. His hair stood up from his scalp in different directions; his ashen skin a stark contrast to his wild and bright eyes; as he walked toward Phil, his legs shook and his hands constantly moved over his clothes and through his hair. He grabbed Phil by the front of his shirt and shook him.

"Where the hell of you been, man? You said you'd be back at eleven!"

"Mark. It is eleven. You're just having a little anxiety attack. Calm down."

"Don't tell me to calm down, you fuck!" Mark yelled in Phil's face. "Where's my shit? *WHERE IS IT?*"

"Uh, technically it's not yours until you pay for it."

Mark's drug-denied system sparked into overload. He slammed Phil against the wall and spat in his face.

"You son of a bitch. You think you can play me? You think you can sweep in and out when you want, bring in your supply, and then deny those of us who need it? You're not gonna get away with this shit. I'm busting your ass to Paula."

"Oooo. I'm so scared, *Narc*."

"And then I'm letting Director Simmons know."

Phil swallowed. Paula was a complete pushover. All he had to do was give her a wink and a smile, and she was in his pocket. Simmons, however, was the real power here. He'd pack Phil's ass off to jail before he could blink. He couldn't have that. Besides the fact that he wouldn't have the breezy lifestyle he'd become accustomed to, Phil really was too pretty for prison and didn't want to be anybody's bitch.

He had to do something fast. Phil held up his hands in defeat.

"Okay, Mark. Okay. You win. I've got your stuff right here."

Phil patted his front pocket. Mark's demeanor changed from raging withdrawal to drooling anticipation. He took a step forward, his eyes glued on the front of Phil's pants, so he didn't see Phil's left fist swing around until it was too late. It connected with Mark's jaw and he went down like a sack of stones.

Phil grabbed Mark by his feet and dragged him to the back of the quad, gagging as he entered Mark's bedroom. The stench of sour sweat, remnants of food and sugary drinks, and the thickness of mold and fungus clogged his nostrils and the back of his throat. Newspapers, napkins, torn books, empty wrappers and pop cans, fast food sacks, dirty laundry, homemade bongs, overflowing garbage bags, used straws. Every available space was covered with trash. It seemed when Mark finished with something, he just dropped it and moved on.

Phil pulled a bandana from his back pocket and tied it around his nose and mouth. Even though Phil and his roommates all had separate bedrooms, he couldn't believe he never noticed the stench earlier. Finally able to breathe with this homemade filter, he grabbed Mark's feet again and continued to clear a path through the debris toward the bed. He managed, with some difficulty, to get Mark up on his bed, and laid him on his back. He looked around at the mounds of garbage and saw what he needed: a small wooden chest locked with a tiny padlock.

He knew Mark hid the key in his dresser, so it was a simple task to get it open. Not so simple to paw his way through the dirty underwear, but he managed to get the key and open the chest without vomiting. This was where Mark kept his hidden drug paraphernalia. His syringes, spoons, lighters, rubber tubing, foil, small pipe-shaped bongs, and anything else he'd need to inject, snort, or smoke drugs.

Phil pulled out a syringe, careful not to prick his fingers on anything. He wasn't afraid of dirty needles or contracting HIV. All the stuff in the chest was new. God only knew what might enter his bloodstream from the bedroom itself, though. He also grabbed a spoon, lighter, and rubber tubing. The heroin was still in Phil's pocket, so he had all he needed for Mark's accidental overdose.

Last month another resident had accidentally overdosed, but when they found him, he was still sitting up on the side of the bed. Whatever he had done had killed him so quickly that when he folded his legs to sit down, he died within seconds of hitting the mattress. He'd been like that for about two days. It wasn't until he missed a counseling appointment that anyone thought something was wrong. Phil tried to prop Mark up the same way, but Mark kept flopping over onto his back.

Thirty minutes later, Phil stood over the body and admired his handiwork. Mark was on his back, a syringe dangling from the crook of his right elbow, the rubber tubing tied into place. Phil placed the dirty spoon on the floor, inches from the bed, so it appeared as if Mark had dropped it once he shot up his fix. Phil pressed his fingers against Mark's neck and was satisfied when he felt no pulse.

He took a deep breath and screamed at the top of his lungs. He ran for the quad door and raced down the stairs. Bursting into the front office, he stood over Paula, gasping for air.

"Paula, oh my God."

Paula blanched as Phil tried to control himself. She came around from behind her desk and urged him to sit down.

"Easy, Phil. Easy does it. Sit down. Now, what's going on?"

"Paula, it's Mark," he gasped. "Oh God, he's, he's-"

"Wait here. I'll be right back."

Paula scuttled down the hall and up the stairs as quickly as her plump little legs could carry her. Once she was out of earshot, Phil stopped having hysterics and picked up a magazine from the side table. He looked up at the ceiling when he heard a distant shout, accompanied by a few pounding footsteps, as people ran from other ends of the center to help Paula with her discovery. Phil smiled and went back to the magazine.

Hours later, after the police, Director Simmons, and several other caseworkers at the center questioned him, Phil closed and locked the door to an empty room down the hall from his usual one. The coroner's office, by law, had to seal off his quad with yellow tape because of possible biological contamination involved with a death. Only Mark's family could give permission to break that seal and let anyone back in the room.

Stretching out on his new bed, Phil smiled. No one doubted the overdose story, not here. It happened all the time. Mark had been on edge lately and suffered from depression. Now he was a statistic. Phil rolled onto his side, but just as he got comfortable, there was a knock at his door.

"Who's there?"

"Sarah."

Phil frowned, wondering what his new quad-mate could want, and shuffled over to the door. He pulled it open a couple of inches and peeked out at her.

"What?"

Though she seemed fragile for her petite frame, she shoved the door open and sent Phil backwards into the room. As he stumbled to right himself, she shut the door and locked it.

"What the hell is your problem?" Phil shouted.

"I know."

"You know what, bitch?"

She bowed her head and looked up at him from beneath long lashes coated in a thick layer of black mascara.

"I *know*, Phil."

His bravado faltered. She smirked, walked over to the couch, and made herself comfortable before clearing her throat.

"I'm a little parched, Phil. Got anything to drink in here?"

"What do you want?"

"You know, iced tea, pop. Maybe a little water?"

He folded his arms over his chest. "No."

"Huh. Just want me to get to the point, eh?"

"That would be preferable."

"You're no fun, Philly. Oh, well. Here's the deal. You cut me in on your, uh, little side business, and I don't go to the cops and tell them you murdered Mark."

Phil's felt the hairs on the back of his neck prickle, but he tried to play it cool.

"I don't know what you're talking about."

"Can't shit a shitter, Phil. Your side business, being the lone supplier of all sorts of yummies for the dregs of this hellhole. I want in."

"You can't prove anything."

Sarah laughed, a bright lilting sound in complete contrast to her Goth exterior. She pulled a small piece of dark grey plastic from her front pocket: a USB drive. She wiggled it in Phil's face. He made a grab for it, but she was too quick.

"Yeah, Mark and I kinda had this penchant for filming ourselves during our 'therapy' sessions. We had cameras hidden all over the quad because, well, let's just say Mark was very acrobatic. One small space was never enough."

Phil gritted his teeth. "What exactly do you want?"

"I want seventy percent of your profits. And I want to be a part of making the deals."

"You must be joking."

She tossed the USB drive from hand to hand, whistling the theme from *Jeopardy*. Phil growled in frustration.

"Sixty percent," Sarah countered.

"Forty-five."

"Fifty. And that's final."

Phil sighed. "Deal."

She tucked the little drive into her pocket. As she headed back out the door, Phil called to her.

"I've got to meet a guy tomorrow to pick up some supplies. I assume you want to be a part of that, too?"

She nodded. "Just let me know when and where and I'll be there."

She patted her pocket to remind him of her leverage. "Don't fuck me over, Phil."

"Oh, I wouldn't dream of it."

The following evening, Phil pounded on Sarah's door. He heard a muffled reply and a minute later, she opened up. A sly grin curled her lip as she closed the door behind her.

"I was beginning to worry about you, Phil. Thought maybe you were going to stab me in the back."

"Who, me? Why, Sarah, I'm crushed."

She laughed, again with a light musical sound that belied her blackmailing, deviant soul. He ground his teeth.

"Let's go. My friend won't wait forever."

As they drove to the outskirts of town, Sarah prattled on and on. She turned out to be the type that couldn't stand silence. Therefore, she filled it with nonsensical trivia, news bits, and group therapy trash. Phil pounded his hand on the steering wheel.

"For Christ's sake, Sarah. Could you just shut up for five fucking minutes? Do I have to listen to your bullshit the whole fucking way?"

She snapped her mouth closed. She turned to look out the window as she chewed her fingernails. If he didn't know better he'd say he hurt her feelings. He cleared his throat.

"Look, Sarah. I'm sorry."

"Hey. No sweat. Don't worry about it. I'm just a junkie whore who's blackmailing you, right?"

He blew out a heavy breath from between his clenched teeth. First he hated her. Now he was feeling sorry for her. Since when did he start pitying people and worrying about their feelings? How did he get himself in this mess? *Being a secret drug-dealing murderer might have something to do with it.* Maybe he should try another line of work. Well, once he finished off Sarah, he'd turn over a new leaf. So much for his newfound sense of sympathy.

He pulled into a rutted driveway and parked the car behind an abandoned house. Sarah scanned the area and grabbed Phil's arm.

"What are you doing? Why are we back here?"

"As unpopulated as this area is, Sarah, we can't risk the cops driving by and finding us before the deal is made, now can we?"

"Yeah, I suppose not."

Phil sighed and opened his door as Sarah exited from her side. He stepped out into the cool night air and took a deep strong breath. Sarah walked up next to him and leaned against the car.

"So, how long before this friend of yours shows up?"

He threw his arm around her shoulders. He felt her tense, but she didn't pull away.

"He'll be here soon enough. In the meantime,"

He tightened his arm around her shoulders and slipped his hand beneath her chin. With a quick hard pull, he snapped her neck and she fell without a sound. Her body crumpled to the ground without complaint, without protest, and without her constant chatter. He felt relief as the weight of worry lifted off his back. Now all he had to do was hide the body and get back to the center before anyone knew they were gone.

He saw the double doors of an old cellar at the base of the house. Dragging Sarah over to them, Phil cursed. She weighed more than she looked. He opened the doors then kicked the body down the cement steps and followed behind. He pulled out a flashlight from his back pocket just as the cellar doors slammed shut. He ran back up the steps, throwing himself against the worn wood. They didn't budge.

"Shit."

He flashed the light behind him to cut through the darkness of the cellar. Rickety wooden shelves leaned left or right under the weight of old mason jars filled with unknown liquids. The dry dirt floor kicked up dust as he walked across it. A narrow set of steps at the far end of the cellar led to a small door. As long as it wasn't locked, Phil might be able to get out of the house that way.

His weight pushed against the wooden steps and each one sagged beneath him. When he reached the door, he grabbed the knob and turned it easily. But the door didn't move. Phil rattled the knob and pushed. *Maybe it's just stuck*, he thought as he threw his weight against it. After three tries the door flew open and he rolled across the floor. As he laid on his back, catching his breath, he realized he was in the kitchen.

Once his breathing returned to normal, he stood. He walked out of the kitchen and into what he supposed was the living room. His flashlight illuminated various pieces of furniture in surprisingly good condition, considering no one had lived here in decades. Just as he focused on a tall cabinet at the far wall his flashlight went out. He hit it against his hand several times, but it didn't even flicker.

As his eyes adjusted to the darkness, he was able to see the front door. When he moved toward it, a dark shape flitted through his peripheral vision. He turned to look, but it was gone. As he did, another form flew past him but he couldn't get a lock on that one either. Each time he turned, another dark shape moved just out of his field of vision until he was spinning in circles. Dizzy, he tripped over his feet and fell on his ass.

When the house stopped whirling, a single shadow moved toward him. Its edges sharpened as it closed in on him. The form solidified into a young girl. She smiled then stepped past him. He studied her bloody feet as she walked by. Several other pairs of feet trailed behind hers and he looked up to see a dozen or more people follow her.

A pretty young woman stood over him and held out her hand. Phil took it and followed her over to a small couch. She guided him to sit down and once he did, she stepped aside to make room for the young girl. Phil watched her as she seemed to glide across the floor. After she sat next to him, the remaining figures surrounded them, their gazes focused on her. She took Phil's hand in her own, her eyes fierce and pitiful at the same time.

"Welcome to eternity, Phil."

EPILOGUE

Travis stared around at the gathered souls before him. His heart ached for many, hardened for others. But he felt a new sense of camaraderie that he'd never felt before. In this house, he was part of a brethren of spirits that were united in their damnation. As twisted as that may seem to his head, his heart fully accepted it. For the first time in his existence, Travis belonged.

He turned to an old man sitting on his right and smiled.

"So, what's your story, old timer?"

Before the man could speak, though, a loud crash echoed from upstairs. The sounds of broken glass trickled down to the group. As one they scattered into the shadows. Minutes later two teenaged boys crept down the main staircase. One shone a flashlight into the dark as the other lit a cigarette.

"This is so cool, Dom. You have the best ideas, man."

The other boy blew a cloud of smoke above his head and nodded his agreement. As they both stepped into the foyer, the shadowy souls bled into the room from the walls, the ceiling, and the floor. The two boys froze in place as they realized they were no longer alone. Travis slithered up behind them, blocking their retreat back upstairs. The others surrounded the youths, wailing and crying their laments.

Tamesin pushed her way through the crowd and stood before the newcomers, her smile showing neither welcome nor warmth. She spread her arms and spoke.

"Welcome to my family home."

ABOUT THE AUTHOR

Peggy Christie is an author of horror and dark fiction. Her work has appeared in dozens of websites, magazines, and anthologies. Her horror fiction/art collaboration, *Plague of Man: SS of the Dead*, can be found through Amazon; her short story collections, *Dark Doorways* and *Hell Hath No Fury*, from Dragons Roost Press; and her vampire novel, *The Vessel*, from Source Point Press. Peggy one of the founding members of the Great Lakes Association of Horror Writers, as well as a contributing writer for the website Cinema Head Cheese. Check out her webpage at themonkeyisin.com for more information on her other publications, and appearances.

Peggy loves Korean dramas, survival horror video games, and chocolate (not necessarily in that order) and lives in Michigan with her husband.

ALSO BY PEGGY CHRISTIE

Hell Hath No Fury

Ever wonder how you might handle a sabbatical from work? Think the bible told you everything there is to know about the Devil? What if the noises coming from under your child's bed weren't just in his imagination? Crack open Hell Hath No Fury, a collection of 21 tales of horror and dark fiction, to learn the answers to these questions. Discover stories of psychotic delusions, ghosts, a murder victim's revenge, and a family brought closer together through torture. All of this and more awaits inside the book you hold in your hands right now.

Dark Doorways

Enter this dark mansion of ghastly delights. Each dark doorway opens to another tale of horror. Some rooms are large banquet halls, others are tiny servant's quarters. Each contains wondrous, fear inducing words from master scribe Peggy Christie. If you have the courage, take hold of one of the latches, open the door......and enter.

ABOUT THE ARTIST

Donald England is a Michigan based artist specializing in creepy and macabre art for the last 25 years. He is a product of late-night eighties television and comic book shops. Over the years, his work has been seen in a number of magazines like *Horror Hound* and *Liquid Cheese*, as well as cover art for Evilspeak. His art has been featured in *Late Night Snack*, *The Thing* and *Stranger Things* art books, *Deadworld* and on the covers of *Erie Tales*, *A Fist full of Dead Folk*, and *Night Pieces*. He is also the co-creator of *Lethal Lita* and *Plague of Man*.

DRAGON'S ROOST PRESS

Dragon's Roost Press is the fever dream brainchild of dark speculative fiction author Michael Cieslak. Since 2014, their goal has been to find the best speculative fiction authors and share their work with the public. For more information about Dragon's Roost Press and their publications, please visit:

Dragon's Roost Press

For more great horror, please check out our new website:

http://www.thedragonsroost.biz

Made in the USA
Columbia, SC
13 May 2024

35289233R00095